SUCKING DEAD

BOOK 4

SUCK IT UP

ANDIE M. LONG

CHAPTER

ONE

Ginny

"Can I have a Glenlivet and your phone number?" the puffy-faced vampire at the bar asked. He'd been turned just after a dental procedure. After the dentist had extracted a tooth and a private fee for two hundred pounds, Cuthbert had decided to nip down the alleyway across from the dental surgery as he felt a little woozy. A few minutes later he was even woozier as Santori Letwine had smelled the blood congealing around the wound and extracted the rest of the blood from his body.

Cuthbert had luck on his side that day however, because Santori was already in deep shit for leaving dead bodies around for other Letwine vampires to clear up, so on that day he decided to turn Cuthbert instead and make himself a new ally.

In contrast, Santori himself did *not* have luck on his side as Edmond Letwine, the elder of the clan, declared him too loose a cannon and had him staked, giving Cuthbert all of Santori's assigned tasks in the clan.

It had led to an inflated cheeked vampire, with an inflated opinion of himself.

"You can have the whisky and pay your tab," I informed him. He'd been annoying me all night and while most of the time I ignored drunk vampires who felt it was okay to flirt with me, taking it as part of the job, tonight I was feeling in a mood. Did this puffa fish imposter think I would really be interested in him? Me, Virginia Letwine? I could only think his inebriation had worked in reverse of how it did for humans, his 'beer goggles' elevating his self-esteem but affecting his eyesight, so he thought I was at his level.

"Oh, come on, baby. Don't be like that. I heard you like money and want a rich man. I'm rich in the pants department if you get my drift, and I'm sure we can work out a way to earn some money. Bet there's a vampire or two here who would pay to spend time with my girl. I could manage you and in return you could give me a percentage of the takings... and the goods."

Everything went red as fury burned through my

veins. I broke off a piece of the bar's wooden counter, leapt over it, and knocked Cuthbert to the floor landing astride his thighs. "Oh, Cuthbert, I'm on top of you, just as you were imagining," I teased. "Now let me see to your dick."

I plunged the stake right through his groin. Whether I could have perforated his tiny dick or either of his balls I couldn't know. I just knew it hurt him. Hurt him a damn lot. I twisted it and watched the vampire below me turn a shade of green. Looked like I could sit on Cuthbert and feel highly satisfied after all.

"I'd rather fuck a poor man than fuck anyone as ugly as you," I whispered, leaning over him. The rest of the patrons of the bar were stood back watching us with interest.

"It's all about appearances with you, isn't it?" my brother said from beside me.

"He's ugly inside and out and he asked if he could be my pimp," I said.

"Yes, well looking at him, I would guess he has no doubt now changed his mind. So could you take out the stake because us men have morning wood, not evening wood."

I pulled it out which meant that any wound would close quickly, and Cuthbert would be an angry vampire within seconds. Anticipating this, Lawrie grabbed him by the neck and pushed him up against the wall, the bloody stake now in his hand.

"You'll take a walk now, sober up, and forget all about this, otherwise I'll place this stake through your heart next time I hear you've been propositioning my sister. Now get out before I change my mind and finish you now."

"Thanks, Lawrie," I said. "He just really icks me out and when he said that—"

A voice came from behind me.

"You should have left the bar and come and found me. I'm the elder of this clan and I would have meted out the necessary punishments," Edmond Letwine said in a low, authoritative tone. While I kept standing up straight, inside I withered when faced with our fierce leader.

"I'm sorry, Edmond," I apologised. "It won't happen again."

"No, it won't, because I'm putting Rune behind the bar in your place. He and Acker can manage things."

I couldn't help it. My hands went to my hips, and I folded my arms across my chest. "So the men in this bar can't behave themselves, but I get punished? I lose my job because they think with their dicks after a drink instead of their brains?"

Edmond sighed, looking at me like you might a child after answering their 'Why' questions all day. "No, Ginny. It's because you've been very short-tempered of late. You need to find a job that makes you feel more restful and relaxed. Something that soothes your soul."

I stared at him. "Has Mya been teaching you meditation again?"

"That is not your concern," he answered. "However, when you next bump into her you might like to ask her for some useful podcasts in managing aggression."

"Cuthbert wanted to be my *pimp*." My voice rose with each uttered word.

"And I would have dealt with his impropriety, Virginia."

Full name alert, I thought. I needed to be careful. I sucked in my lips so I couldn't say anything else. Made myself listen and look attentive.

"Now, however, you've taken matters into your own hands, literally by twisting a stake in his penis, and that means his punishment is already served and I cannot sanction anything further against him. Indeed, what you've done is give him leverage to come to me about *you*."

"If I am to be punished, then let me know because

I'll go and finish him off," I snarled. If I was going down, I was taking Fuckbert with me. All thoughts of calm were lost as my fangs descended and I knew my eyes would be blazing red.

"No punishments, other than you're fired," Edmond said. "And you're to keep away from Cuthbert. Either find that nice job we spoke about, or take a sabbatical, but either way you need to learn to chillax. Is that understood, Virginia, because I have other much more pressing things to deal with."

"Yes, Sir."

"Excellent. Good evening, Lawrie. I shall expect you to oversee your sister's rehabilitation," he added, and then he vanished, having no doubt whizzed off to his 'pressing matters', which knowing Edmond was his ironing. He was obsessed with a 'traveller's crease' in all his trousers.

I turned to Lawrie. "You don't have to babysit me. I'll behave."

Lawrie tilted his head towards me. "You have been sullener and more irritable of late. What's going on with you?" he asked.

I went behind the bar, took a bottle of vodka and indicated towards the door. Acker could do the rest of the shift on his own and have my middle finger as payment for the bottle of Absolut in my hand. I was done with The Vampire's In(n).

We left the dark bar and entered the soft summer night. There was a gentle breeze as we strolled across the grounds towards the Letwine mansion.

"I'm fed up with everyone," I confessed. "You're all too goddamn happy. I can't cope with it. It makes me want to throw up in my mouth or shove a stake through my own heart."

"What?" Lawrie's mouth dropped open. "So basically, what you're saying is that you are in dire need of a good shag?"

"That too," I huffed. "But I'm an evil vampire, Lawrie, and you were too, and now look at you. You work in a café selling pink glittery cupcakes and kiss your wife every five seconds while declaring your love." I pulled a grimace.

"That's because I'm in love. As Climie Fisher said, '*Love Changes (Everything)*'."

I cast my eyes down to his groin area. "Where's another stake when you need one?"

"Look. Go be miserable in your room for the night. Make a Cuthbert voodoo doll or whatever you need to do. Watch *The Craft* on repeat. But tomorrow morning, come to the café. Spend some time with the girls. You always feel better when you've seen Dela."

Dela was my friend, but she was also madly in love. Her advice now came covered in a smothering of bliss. However, she still was a good friend, and I did like hanging around the bookstore.

"Okay. I'll come around in the morning," I agreed.

"Excellent, I'll see you then. It will all work out okay, Ginny. You'll see. If I can end up with Callie, then miracles do truly happen."

That made me smile.

"A smile? Oh my goodness, be careful there. You'd better immerse yourself in revenge witchcraft before you lose your bitchcraft."

He'd whizzed away before he got to see my raised middle finger, which was getting plenty of action tonight, even if neither I nor Cuthbert was.

As a vampire we needed little sleep, so after a power hour, and catching up on some TV programmes I'd recorded, the next morning I set off for Books and Buns, my sister-in-law's café and bookstore. Travel was a piece of piss as a vampire. I thought of my destination and whizzed straight there.

Callie looked pleased to see me and I soon found

there was another reason for it apart from her hubby having ordered me there.

"Ginny, any chance you can give me a hand with the shop this morning?" she said. So much for the red velvet cupcake and pink lemonade I'd been hoping for, but there was a queue forming and no sign of either Dela or Aria.

"Sure," I said. "I'll run the bookstore. Where is everyone?"

"Dela's no doubt in bed, and Aria is sick. She's been vomiting all morning apparently."

I froze. Vampires didn't vomit. In the back of my mind were Merrin's words from last year. Then a customer asked a question and I pushed it all to the back of my mind.

Jason entered the store. He was Dela's boyfriend's best friend, but I remembered him more from being an onlooker when the great undead and unwashed had talked to me like crap. God knows what he was doing being a friend to that... *thing*. One day I would make Merrin suffer, because I'd not forgotten that day when he'd talked to me with such disdain. How dare he act superior to me. Me! I was a Letwine vampire who lived in a mansion in luxury, and he was a zombie who I believed lived in a reclamation yard which I doubted had washroom facilities given the state of him.

Jason's phone rang and I watched as his expression changed to one of panic and he shouted out, "Oh shit."

"What's the matter, Jason?" Callie asked, rushing to his side.

"Ali at the yard has just called. A load of the junk Merrin had stored has just collapsed and Merrin is buried under it all. He can't die from it as he's already dead, but Merrin is extremely claustrophobic. We have to rescue him as quickly as possible. I need Nick and his expertise. Maybe he can use his digger to help?" he suggested.

"There's no need," I said, stepping forward. "Tell me where exactly this place is and I shall go there immediately. I can easily rescue him using my superior vampire strength."

"Er, if you're sure..."

"I'm beyond sure. It would be my pleasure to help him," I declared.

And as Jason reeled off his address and I got ready to whizz over there, I smirked. It would indeed be my pleasure when I removed the crap covering Merrin and he saw just who had rescued him.

He'd be appalled.

And that made my dead heart very happy indeed.

It looked like Lawrie's idea of me coming to work here today had been an excellent one. I could hang with my friends in the shop, plus torment the life out of Merrin for my entertainment. Well, he was dead, but you knew what I meant.

'Let's go then," I said, and I grabbed hold of Jason and whizzed us both to the yard.

CHAPTER TWO

Merrin

My yard was once again being swamped by Gnarly's excess furniture. I was going to have to bring this up at the next council meeting because it seemed the residents of our small village weren't sticking to the 'reduce, re-use, recycle' mantra as much as they once had been. They felt donating their pieces to me for repurposing meant they could buy whatever they wanted and feel they'd done their bit by not throwing it away for the bin men for landfill.

No, it was my land becoming full. Every so often I'd get a large project like when I'd been asked to provide the furniture for Dela Francis' new home, and I'd think I could get a handle on my stock, but then another resident would give their place a makeover and another van full of their unwanted furniture would arrive.

Don't get me wrong, I loved to work on these pieces: restoring, re-purposing, etc, but each piece took time and so more came in than went back out. Even taking on another guy, Alistair, as an apprentice and then showing him how to set up his own business hadn't made much more of a dent in moving stock.

I loved seeing the beauty in things, yet all I could see when I looked out of the window of my small one-bedroomed cottage were the piles of unwanted rubbish; when, with a little gardening expertise, I could have a nice plot outside my house that looked over views of the woodland.

Something most definitely had to change. But in the meantime, I had to get a bureau out from under a few other piled up things as that was what I was working on today. Fenella who worked at the laundry wanted to start writing a Christmas book apparently. Since she lived with Santa, I guessed she had the inside track, but it was June and as the heat of the morning picked up, it was hard for me to think about the festive season.

I thought fondly of last Christmas though. Dela's home had been finished and her boyfriend Nick, a friend of mine, had invited me along for dinner as part of the surprise reveal. Given I'd always been very fond of my own company, I found, rather surprisingly to me, that I'd liked being around the other guests, eating good food and enjoying a beer. It had created a feeling of emptiness within me since. I felt unsettled and had this gut feeling that something big was coming: a change, but also... danger. I hated these 'gut feelings' or 'knowings' because I was generally correct and so I'd spent the last week or so with a feeling of foreboding accompanying me all day and night.

I watched as Alistair's van came up the driveway, the gravel crunching under his tyres, and I went outside to greet him.

"Morning, Merrin," he said, with a wave as he excited his vehicle.

"Morning, Alistair. You come to pick up another piece?"

"Yeah." Alistair smiled. He was older than me, forty to my thirty, but we got along just fine. He and his wife, Terri, had recently had a baby and while Terri went back to work, Alistair was a stay-at-home dad, doing his furniture business during the evenings and in the rare snatches of peace he got in between. And he said he didn't get many of those with a newborn.

"Can you help me get this bureau out while you're

here?" I asked. "Only I want to get started on it this morning."

"Sure." He looked over at the piled-up furniture. "Please don't tell me it's in that lot," he said, pointing to the largest stack over in the disused cowshed where my gaze kept landing.

I shrugged.

"Shit. We've got to do something about this place, Merrin. It's a death trap."

"I know. I'm going to raise it at the next council meeting. The villagers of Gnarly must do better."

"Good. Glad to hear it. I'll make sure I'm there to back you up."

"Appreciated."

"Okay then, let's get this bureau out and while we take the other pieces down, I'll see if I can find my own next project."

"Cheers, Alistair. I'm glad you showed up today."

I was even more pleased he was there after what happened next.

Metalwork items and other such things were outside the front of my house, covered in waterproof tarpaulin where needed, but the rest stood inside the disused cowshed. That was where we walked over to now, and we began to move bits of the stacked furniture.

"Let's put the pieces out here separately and then when we've moved your bureau and whatever I choose to one side, we can stack the rest in a more thought-out manner," Alistair suggested.

"Sounds like a plan," I agreed.

I heard Alistair as he walked away, saying he was going to get the ladder so we could get to the top, but I reached over to the pile where there was a small table at the side. I could be moving that.

It all happened in slow motion. As if playing unwanted furniture Jenga, as I took the piece out, I knocked the piece next to it. There was a wobble, and I took a deep breath that it would stop.

The next thing I knew was the pile began sliding towards me, forming a brand-new pile as it shifted sideways with me now underneath it all.

"Oh my fucking god, Merrin, are you okay?" Alistair's panicked voice came from outside of the now rearranged pile of goods.

"I'm not injured. I'm a zombie, remember? Already dead. However." I started to scrunch up my eyes and put my hands in my hair. "I am claustrophobic."

I realised then that I was at the bottom of a pile of

wooden goods and couldn't get out. Trapped. It was like being in the grave again. The items my wooden coffin, and me having to punch my way out. I tried to calm myself, chanting, "It's not the same. You're fine. You're fine." But the memories began to assail me again and the darkness closed in.

I screamed. "Alistair, help meeeeee."

I heard Alistair's voice asking for help, though it was muted due to the furniture lying over me. How long would they take to get here though? They might as well also send a psychiatric doctor along with the rescue team because I'd need them by then.

So imagine my surprise when not two minutes later I heard Alistair shouting to me that I'd be out shortly, and then I could hear things moving. Not one minute later I was uncovered, and I caught sight of my rescuer... Virginia Letwine.

Oh God no. Anyone but her. *She'd* rescued me? The spoiled brat vampire. How had she ended up here?

"Well, good morning, Merrin. I'll let your friends check you over, because I certainly won't be going near enough to you to do so, and then I'll wait for your thanks." She stood to the side while Alistair and Jason came closer.

"Cover me back up with all the furniture," I yelled. "Having to thank her is worse than the claustrophobia."

I heard her snigger.

"Are you okay, mate?" Jason said, as Alistair helped me to my feet.

"Define okay," I snapped. "Physically I'm fine. I don't bruise or get badly hurt as I'm dead already. However, my mental health has been severely compromised by being in the enclosed space and facing the fact I've been rescued by *her*."

"What is your problem with Ginny?" Jason whispered. "And stop being so snappy with me when I'm the reason you got rescued so quickly. Ginny was in the café when Alistair called, and her vamp strength meant you were out in super quick time."

"There's no point in whispering," Ginny said. "Super strength hearing also, remember?"

"Right, well, I don't know what has gone on between you guys and why you have this hate thing going on. I can't work out whether it's dislike or if you want to jump the other one's bones hard. Is it hate or intense sexual chemistry?"

"Hate," we both said in unison.

"But why?"

"She's made it clear that the only men of any worth to her are rich ones, which she will use to gain shiny, pretty things. She uses people and has no regard for their welfare. I loathe her kind," I informed Jason.

"He's high and mighty and all holier than thou, when he doesn't know me at all. He's just judged me from the small amount of time he has seen me. His attitude stinks as much as he does, and that is a *lot*," Ginny countered.

"I don't smell. I wash myself at least once a day given I work with chemicals," I protested.

"Well, the look of you makes me imagine a smell when I see you. All old and fusty and like boiled cabbage."

"Okay then, glad I got that cleared up," Jason said. "Hate it is. That's what you're both saying anyway. Personally, I—"

"Want to be drained?" Ginny asked Jason.

"Oh, I realise I have somewhere to be, so I'm going to leave now," Jason said, and he began walking off the premises. Alistair chose a piece of furniture and left shortly afterwards. That left me, and Ginny, who was still standing staring at me.

"You're not going to leave until I say thank you, are you?" I asked resignedly.

"Nope." She rubbed her hands together and then chuckled unpleasantly.

Realising the sooner I got it over with, the sooner she'd leave, I quickly said, "Thanks, Ginny," before walking towards the bureau which I noticed was now at the bottom of a stacked pile of four pieces of furniture. As she'd rescued me, she must have stacked these back up. There was no way I could touch the stack. Not today. I needed time to process what had happened to me when I was alone again.

Ginny appeared at the side of the pile. "Oh, I think you can say thank you to me a lot more sincerely than that."

"No, actually, I don't think I can," I said with total honesty, wondering if I was prepared to sacrifice a piece of the furniture to make stakes. It was getting closer to a yes with every word she said.

She reached out to touch the pile.

"What are you doing?" I shrieked.

She stopped, holding her hands against her ears.

"VAMPIRE HEARING, REMEMBER?" she shouted.

"You don't have to shout. I'm not the one with my hands over my ears."

She took them down. "What on earth was that noise you made?"

"I'm a zombie. It's a zombie cry."

"It's hideous."

"You're hideous."

Her eyes narrowed. "No, I am not. I am amazing actually, and I saved you today and I deserve a thank you for it."

She wasn't going to go away unless I made an attempt at a genuine apology, so it was best I got on with it. It couldn't be worse than being under the pile of rubble, and hopefully I'd be able to avoid seeing her again for a very long time.

"Thank you very much for coming over here so quickly and removing the furniture from me. I'm claustrophobic and so your vampire speed and strength meant I was only under there for a short amount of time. I am therefore truly grateful and thank you from the bottom of my heart for all you have done today."

"God, if you weren't already dead that would have killed you, right?" Ginny laughed and just for a moment she seemed quite normal. "You owe me now, Merbin. That's what I'm going to call you now because you make me think of rubbish."

"And I will call you Ninny for you are a complete nincompoop."

"That the best you've got?" She laughed and

whizzed away, after first taking the furniture down quickly. She'd seen my weakness then when I'd been looking at it. It made me want to scream once more.

"For now. But just you wait," I said out loud. "I'll even things up in time."

✤ CHAPTER ✤
THREE

Ginny

"Sorry about that. I'm back here to help now," I told Callie as I re-appeared in the shop.

"Hey, Ginny. I'm here too now. I'll go back to the café side if you come cover the bookshop," Dela said.

"Will do." The café was bustling, and business looked good. I wasn't surprised. A lot of Gnarly loved reading. Coupling that with buns and hot beverages meant they couldn't stay away. It amused me given I'd rather watch TV and didn't need to eat. And then Callie brought me over a special red-velvet cupcake and a pink lemonade. The secret ingredient in both was o-neg and as I bit on a piece of the bun, at that moment I would have sworn preference over food in my mouth to cock any day of the week. Not that a male had been near my mouth in months.

"So what happened over at Merrin's?" Callie asked, telling people at the counter she'd be back in a minute.

I gleefully told them my tale of rescuing Merrin and making him apologise. Callie then returned to the counter while Dela stayed to chat.

"I don't understand why you don't like him. He's a nice guy. Poor bloke having claustrophobia and being trapped under the furniture like that." Dela's forehead creased. "I might pop by after work with a goody bag from the café for him."

I rolled my eyes. "You haven't been subject to his uncalled-for rudeness. He helped you furnish your house. Of course you can't understand why I don't like him. But what if he'd said you were spoiled and only interested in a rich man?"

Dela sucked her lips in.

"Come on, out with what you want to say?" I huffed.

"It's just that, it's true. You tell everyone you want a rich guy, and you actively seek them out at the Inn," Dela answered.

"*Sought* out at the bar, past tense. It won't be happening again."

"Oh, have you changed your mind?"

"No, I've been fired."

Dela's jaw dropped. "You got *fired*? When? How?"

"Last night. Stupid vampire offered to be my pimp, so I staked him through his cock. Edmond fired me and told me I needed to go find something that would calm me down. Staking Cuthbert through the heart next would have made me feel fabulous, but that's not what he meant. Mya has my leader on all new age woo-woo crap and so he wants me to chant or some shit."

"That's brilliant," Callie said after dropping two teacakes off at a neighbouring table. Dela and I turned to her, my face no doubt wearing the same 'Wtf?' expression as Dela's.

"You like all the woo-woo stuff too?" Dela asked her sister.

"Oh not that. I meant Ginny having been fired. It's just that while you were out, I heard from Aria and she's not going to be back for a while. So, Ginny, would you like to manage the bookstore for the next few months?" Callie asked.

"She's pregnant, isn't she?" I asked in return.

"It's not my news to announce."

"Fuck, he was right," I managed to get out through gritted teeth.

Resting my elbows on the table, I put my head in

my hands. Dela squeezed my shoulder. She'd been there that day. When Merrin was working here getting the shelving and other furniture ready for the revamped café and he'd said that I'd be working here in June when the other fell 'with child'.

"It's not a bad thing that he was right, is it? I mean, you're going to be working here which is much nicer than dealing with inappropriate drunks, and Aria is having a baby. That's something to be celebrated, isn't it?" Dela said.

I sighed and looked up. "I know, but it means he was *right*, and that means he's going to *gloat*."

"Merrin hardly ever comes here. He's too busy on his land. You'll be fine. Please, let's celebrate the fact you're working here." Dela squeezed my hand.

I tore off a piece of cupcake and enjoyed the taste of blood in my mouth. I couldn't even drain Merrin if I wanted to because zombies didn't have any blood. Anyway, I didn't want to picture any part of him in my mouth. Ugh. I pushed away the rest of the cupcake, having completely put myself off it now. My eyes went over to all the books and the cute little corner which would be mine to rule. My little piece of paradise, even if the shelving and counters had all been put in by smelly Merbin.

"When do you want me to start?" I asked Callie,

who was now bustling past clearing tables and looking at Dela wearing a 'Can you fucking work now?' expression.

"You were helping me today anyway, so now?" she raised her eyes expectantly. "And I mean right now, because I'm running around like a headless chicken while you two are sat clucking like mother hens."

"Okay. Yes, I would very much like the job," I said, and Dela squealed.

"Fantastic. Right, ladies, get to work," Callie ordered.

"Do you have any cleaning products?" I asked her.

Callie's mouth downturned. "My shop is spotless."

I nodded. "Spotless yes, Merbin's fingers-touched-less, no. I want to make sure I've cleaned out every possible trace of him."

Callie looked skyward.

"Are you praying?" I asked her.

"You're becoming maniacally obsessed with Merrin," Dela said. "It's weird. Go concentrate on selling books and become obsessed with that instead."

I realised then that my behaviour could look odd to those who didn't know me well.

"I'm not crazy. I'm a vampire. We stalk our prey. It's in my very nature to become obsessed with that I wish to torment."

"Are you saying Merrin is a future victim? That you might *kill* him?" Dela enquired, her voice a few octaves higher than her usual tone.

"God, no. He's so useless he doesn't even have blood. However, the playing with pets is almost as much fun as the killing of them, so he can be a little project for me to mess with. I'll make his life as miserable as possible until he begs me to leave him be."

"Remind me to never piss you off." Dela laughed. "Although, you know, there's a fine line…"

"Between best friends and my fangs going rogue?" I batted my lashes a few times while giving her a fake grin.

She mimed zipping across her lips. "Come on, let's get back to work," Dela said. "Before my sister has a meltdown."

Nodding, I stood and made my way over to the bookshop side of the shop and walked behind the counter. The till was similar to the one I used at the pub, and I already knew that the books were all priced up, with easily removable stickers on the back cover. Just like a satisfied woman in the bedroom, no one wanted a sticky residue left behind on them. Everything else I needed, like the recycled paper and card bags to put purchases in, plus the re-usable cotton totes with book quotes on, were at the rear of my counter.

In no time at all I was selling books and I discovered that not only did I enjoy the feeling of selling, but also hearing people chat about their favourite books. I suddenly began to understand Aria's obsession with the written word. I ended up buying myself one of the books recommended by another customer and looked forward to going back to the mansion and reading.

After I'd been to see my friend that is, to celebrate her news—once I'd wheedled it out of her.

The Letwine mansion was vast and the vampires all had suites of varying sizes depending on how many of them shared. Some of them were like frat houses and Edmond wisely split the males living that way and put them in a wing at one end, and any lone females at the other. With couples or larger mixed or settled groups in the middle in bigger suites, it was the best way of dividing up the upper floor. We had bedrooms even though we slept little. They were more for fornication. I considered changing my bedlinen to a sand colour given my bed action was as parched as a desert.

Closing the door behind me, I made my way to Aria and Bernard's suite. Only when I got there, I found there was a queue. Huh, looked like the news was already out. A vampire called Imelda was at the head of the queue, getting people to stay in line. I strolled up to the front.

"Waiting time is approximately four hours and you get ten minutes," Imelda said. "I can give you a ticket and you can come back if you prefer?"

"Are you fucking kidding me? I have to wait to see my own friend?"

"Not kidding. Do you have any idea how rare this is? Once news gets out further than the mansion, there'll be more vampire clans wanting to pass on their regards other than the Letwine vampires. Aria will be treated as a god or a lucky charm. People will wish to touch her, to see if they may be afforded the same luck."

"I'd like to see them try to touch her," I mumbled under my breath.

Right on cue, the door opened, and a vampire named Romilly sailed through it landing on her arse at the other side of the hall.

She stood up and shook herself down.

"I did warn you," Imelda told her.

"I only tried to reach for a thread of cotton she had hanging off her cardigan. Crazy lunatic almost staked me with her elbow," Romilly complained.

While Imelda was distracted chatting to Romilly, I

snuck into the room. I heard a "Hey," behind me, but it was too late. I closed the door and made my way to the living room to see my friend.

"If one more person tries to touch me, Bernard, so help me God, I will drain them."

I sauntered through the door and saw Aria visibly relax. "Thank fuck, someone normal. Did you have to queue?"

I scoffed. "I love you, but I queue for no one. I did what all British hate, vampire or not, I queue-jumped; so if I'm never seen again, there will be at least twenty-three suspects, all of whom arc currently outside bitching about me to Imelda."

Bernard (pronounced according to him as Bair-nnaarrd) was my brother's best friend and via that connection I'd become good friends with his wife. Also, she was one of the few female vampires I had time for. I found most extremely dull. Most vampire dudes, being as pathetic as they were, tended to turn their 'perfect woman', which half the time was a brain-dead, big-boobed, Barbie doll lookalike. Turning super-sized a lot of things, but boobs and brain cells weren't among them.

"Would you like an o-neg?" Bernard asked.

"Yes please, I'd love one," I answered, more for the fact I wanted him out of the room, than for the fact I was thirsty.

As soon as he was out of vampire earshot, I turned to my friend.

"So it's true? You're pregnant?" I leaned over and gave her a massive hug and then sat down next to her on the sofa. "Tell me all. Well, except for how it got there. I can work that out for myself."

"I felt so sick." Aria stroked her belly. "It was so bad, and I had these strange pains in my stomach. Bernard became concerned and called the doctor, who was stunned when he worked out what the cause was. Unfortunately, not so stunned that he couldn't keep his mouth shut. So much for patient confidentiality. He ran to tell Edmond, and said it rather too loudly, and we know what our kinds hearing is like. Hence the queues outside with people wanting to pass on their best regards. I mean, I'm maybe a month pregnant they reckon, and I'll be pregnant for another six. I'm due December 25th, which means I don't need to buy Bernard a Christmas gift this year, I'm going to launch his present right out of my vagina."

"Thanks for that visual," I told her. "Hey, listen,

you know that weirdo who made the furniture at the bookshop, the one who was mean to me?"

"Merrin?"

"Yeah. Well, he's a lot strange and reckons he has these 'knowings' and he said you'd get pregnant in June and that I'd work at the shop. The twat was right."

Aria's eyes went wide. "And you didn't warn me?"

I lifted both my hands, palms up. "I thought he was being ridiculous, and I didn't want you getting your hopes up. There hasn't been a vampire birth for fifteen years."

"Okay, I get that. It's been quite a shock though. I just hope I'm not going to be hounded day and night for the rest of my days. I can't stand most of them, Ginny." She lowered her voice. "I wish we could move to Gnarly, away from them all."

"What?!" I exclaimed. "Leave Chelsea?"

"Sssh." Aria put a finger to her lips. "I don't want anyone out there hearing. But listen, your brother lives there now, and not only does Bernard miss him, but I have him bugging me more because he's bored. It's how I've ended up pregnant in the first place. Wouldn't it be fabulous if me and Bernard, and you of course, could go live there away from all these idiots?

Gnarly is so much more interesting than this Dullsville."

"But you have to apply to reside in Gnarly and you need to find a house. I mean, Dela got that rare spot in the woods to do a new build, but only because there was no chance of anything being grown on it due to the fungus there."

"There must be some room somewhere." Aria sighed in frustration.

That was when I thought of exactly where there was room. Where a certain annoying male had far too much land that he wasted opportunity on by having it piled high with trash.

"What? You have that look on your face. The one you get when you set your eye on a new rich guy. That intense focus."

I tapped my finger against my lips. "I've thought of a possibility, but it needs further research. I don't know who owns the land or how I could get permission for us to build there. Leave it with me for a while. But yes, it would be incredible if we could move to the fell."

Aria reached over and squeezed me. "Oh, this is so exciting. What a day. Finding out I'm pregnant and maybe getting a new home in a lovely little village."

"Well, I don't know if my idea will work yet."

"Oh, let a woman dream. I can think about it while I suffer through the rest of these visitors."

I laughed and then Bernard came back with my drink. We talked more about their surprise and delight about the baby, and my new job, and then I left them to the rest of their evening, receiving visitors.

Back in my own room, I changed into some comfy loungewear and settled back on my chaise with my new book, but I found myself distracted, thinking of potentially living in Gnarly.

I needed to find out if Merrin owned that land and if he did, how to get half of it off him so we could build a house out there for Aria and Bernard, and another for me. And a huge brick wall that separated us from Smelly Merry.

Merrin

Jason called me later that afternoon. "Oh, you answered. Thought you might be balls deep by now."

"Balls deep into tidying up the mess over here?" I suggested, even though I knew exactly what he was getting at.

"What is it with you and her? It's weird. I've never come across anything like it and believe me I've had my share of women who don't like me... more than my share in fact."

I knew why I hated Ginny. It was about what she represented. Treating men like a way of gaining wealth and status. I'd been there, done that, in my past, and it had led to such tragedy that I detested anyone who thought it was a way to get on in life. People had feelings, and I had more than most. Risen from the grave, I'd found myself 'sensitive', and at times when my calling was at its loudest—spirits chatting in my ears or sending me images and pictures—I had to retire to my plot of land and hunker down until I got it all under control.

But today, my place of safety had become a place of danger, and *that woman* had been on my land.

"She just irks me, that's all. All that pursuing men for their money. Anyway, was that the only reason you were calling?"

"No, I wondered if you fancied coming out for a beer and a burger? It's a nice night and so the bistro has the tables out in the boulevard. Thought you might fancy a drink after your adventures today."

"Sounds good. I'll meet you there in what, half an hour?" I suggested. Being here was just making me focus on the mess and the fact it felt polluted by Ginny having wandered around. The place needed an exorcism: both to banish a certain female vampire from ever coming here again, and the masses of recycling.

She got you out of there super-fast, my mind chided. *That was a good thing, even if she did it to be smug.*

Now I knew why I disliked her, but why did she hate me so much? She said I made her think of the 'great unwashed'. Hmmm. I decided I'd go find an old, abandoned mirror and take a good look at myself. Not that I gave a crap what she thought, but I did what some others thought. I didn't want to look a mess while out with my friend.

"Make it an hour," I told Jason, and I went in search of my reflection.

From an objective point of view, I didn't exactly rock the look of a hot, sex god. After wiping the dusty full-length mirror with a cloth, I'd stood in front of it and turned this way and that, taking an overall look at myself.

My hair was long and straggly. My body looked waif-like due to the fact I picked up my clothes from *Seconds the Best* and deliberately chose baggy because I thought it hid my slim shape, Instead, it accentuated it. I'd grown a beard and it made my face look elongated and therefore even thinner.

Truth was, I'd never given a toss about my appearance, because I felt beauty was skin deep. But now, as I stared at myself, I felt like I had a point to prove to the vacuous new bookstore assistant. I'd improve my appearance and then if she treated me differently, I'd call her out on it in front of everyone. Show them just how judgemental she was and fixed on looks. She was also fixed on wealth, but we'd ignore that part for now.

Either I'd get Ginny to have a huge personality transplant, or I'd drive her back to the Letwine mansion. But there was no way she was staying in Gnarly as was, poisoning the place with her petty personality.

Not on my watch.

No one else had ever judged me here or insulted me. I was accepted as I was. As a zombie. Gnarly was made of different supernaturals, and our true forms were all different shapes and sizes. Hell, my friend Jason was a dragon! I suppose if Ginny saw his true self, she'd want him to apply a shit ton of Crème de la Mer on his scales because they were too dry and scaly for her eyes to look upon.

And while I tidied myself up to prove a point to her, I'd also tidy my place up so that I might actually get myself the home I craved. It was time to remind the villagers of Gnarly to make better choices other than to overwhelm my land. I needed space, mentally and physically.

I walked away from the mirror, grabbed my wallet, and set off to the bistro. Right now, I was going to enjoy a pint and a burger with my friend. A man who liked me exactly for who I was.

|

"Man, I need to get laid," Jason said as he drank down his third pint.

"There's a film about you, isn't there? *The 40-year-old Virgin*."

"Piss off, I'm only twenty-nine."

He didn't say he wasn't a virgin because after a prank last summer in a hotel room, Jason had admitted to being exactly that. And despite his best intentions, nothing had changed since.

"It's not like I don't get hit on. Women are always coming up to me, but then I take them on a date, and it all goes wrong."

It was true. While ever we were out together, females tended to look at him rather than me. Any women I'd met were usually goth chicks from if Jason and I headed to London for the night. And there hadn't been many for me either. Just one-night stands that had taken the edge off. No repeats because I liked being a loner, and not having to explain my weirdness to people.

"Jase?"

"Yeah?"

"How come you hang out with me? Like, given I'm a bit weird?"

He spluttered his beer. "A bit weird? Try majorly freaking weird."

"Gee, thanks."

He answered in his typical, completely open and honest Jason way. "You're fun when people get to know you. When you let down your guard. And if you're being stranger than usual, I know there's a reason behind it because I've known you for ages. I mean, you're aware I can be snappy and bad-tempered due to my inner dragon. If I'm being like that you call me on it, tell me to go off and calm down. It's what mates do."

"Cool. That makes sense. Thanks."

"Plus, the fact you look such a state means more babes look at me than you."

It was my turn to splutter my beer.

"I'm joking, Merrin. You have that whole emo thing going on. Some chicks dig that. As we know by the fact you aren't in living in Neverland."

"What's Peter Pan got to do this this?"

"Funny. Okay, Neverdoneitland. I was trying not to say it so plainly while out in public. You never know who's listening."

"That's so true." Mya walked past, grabbing a chair from a neighbouring table and sitting down next to us. "So you've not done it... ever?"

"Mya!" Her boyfriend, Death, fixed her with a glare.

"Oh go and get me a pina colada and leave me a moment," said the Queen of Wayward Souls.

"It's okay." Jason waved Death off.

"Well, I won't be long. Queues tend to disappear quickly when I'm around." Death smirked and walked off.

"Have you heard of manifesting?" Mya asked Jason.

He shook his head. "Nope." He gave me a quick look of 'help', but I sat back to nurse the rest of my pint and to enjoy his discomfort.

"Basically, you have to keep a positive energy around you while acting as if you already have what you want. Then you'll attract what you want."

"Come again?"

"Say I want some more Louboutins. To attract them I keep positive and then I'll find a pair appears."

Death had returned with Mya's drink and he placed it on the table. "I don't think the fact you're sometimes extra nice to me when you want a new pair of shoes is quite manifesting, darling."

"I can always have a strop," she said, following it up with a fake smile.

"Do take a look online and see if there are any others you'd like, my sweet. Especially ones with a nice heel."

"He likes me to walk on his back in them. It turns him on," she said.

Death put his death mask on to cover up his embarrassment and then he disappeared.

"I'll be in the bad books now for talking about our sex life again, so I'd better go make amends. And by make amends I mean shag him. I'm sorry you've not got any yet, Jason. Once you start, you'll realise what you've been missing."

Jason groaned and I wasn't sure if it was through pain or embarrassment.

Mya zoomed off in that way vampires did, where one minute they were there and the next not. They were sneaky buggers due to their super-hearing, super-speed, and super-strength. Suddenly, my mind was back on Ginny and how quickly she'd moved my furniture. It had made me feel emasculated as she'd gloated about rescuing me.

"What am I going to do?" Jason pleaded, as Chantelle, a waitress from the bistro came to collect our glasses. She was a witch, although at times her magic went wrong.

"Can you perform a spell on Jason so he can get laid, Chantelle?" I asked her, half-joking. The bubbly blonde giggled.

"I can't make someone sleep with him, but I can do something to make him show his best self?"

"Yeah, that'll do."

"Hey, I'm right here!" Jason protested.

"Do you want to attract more women?" I asked.

"Yes."

'Well then."

He sighed. "Okay, Chan. Whatever you can do to assist."

She faffed around, magically clearing the space around us and then she closed her eyes and faced him.

To try too hard, can repel.
So, Goddess, I ask you to please heed this spell.
To attract for this man, his perfect mate.
The one who would be sent by fate.
No matter the action, let true love win through.
Despite frustration your one shall come to you.

"All done," she said. "That should do the trick. Good luck, Jason." She smiled and then she high fived me on her way past.

"Oh bugger," she said, coming back two minutes later. "I didn't close the spell."

"Is that a problem?" Jason asked. "Have you ruined my love life instead of saved it?"

I was tempted to query how you could ruin something non-existent, but instead turned to Chantelle, concerned she'd messed up yet another spell.

"I just need to close it now, that's all. The worst that could happen is it spread to you," she said to me matter-of-factly. "I'd drawn a protective circle around the table."

She closed down the spell while my mind whirred.

"All done now," she confirmed.

"Are you saying the spell could have been cast on me also?" I double checked.

"It's unlikely because I was focused on Jason, but if it did, it will just encourage the future love of your life to appear if you have one. It's gonna happen anyway. This is just a small kick up the bum for fate."

I felt a bit jittery. Was I ready for that? To meet a woman who might like me for me?

Oh fuck it, Merrin. It was probably the four pints I'd now drunk dulling my brain cells' thinking capabilities, but Chantelle went on her way, and I decided to leave the unlikely, but possible spell in place.

At that point Milly and Tilly, the twins wandered over to us.

"Can we sit with you? Only there are no other tables. I just need to grab one other chair," Tilly said.

"Allow me," Jason said gallantly. He'd been very subservient to them ever since he'd tried to trick them into a threesome last year. That had resulted in mine and Nick's prank which had led to Jason's admission of intact virginity. The twins had forgiven him. They didn't have it in them to be nasty and Jason wasn't a sleaze, just misguided.

As they sat down with us, Jason looked over at me with a nod towards them. A nod that clearly asked, 'Do you think these two might be our true loves?'

I hadn't the foggiest, so I just shrugged and let the evening go where it may.

After another couple of hours, I'd learned one thing. My true love wasn't here. Both Milly and Tilly were lovely, but I wasn't attracted to either of them.

They'd been telling us about how Chantelle had worked with her mentor Alicia to perform a spell that meant they could now talk independently of one another.

"So, we will hopefully be able to live separate lives, but while remaining sisters and the best of friends," Milly explained.

"That sounds like excellent news," I replied.

"So what's happening with you, Merrin?" Tilly asked. "You seem okay, but I heard you were in an accident earlier today?"

"Oh, it was nothing really." I dismissed it. "Actually though, I want to come see the two of you tomorrow to discuss second-hand furniture as I need a plan of what to do with everything I have. Might need some contacts from you."

"Of course. Pop in anytime. We'll be in from ten." Tilly giggled.

"We'll need to sleep off our hangovers," Milly explained.

A table became free, and the twins excused themselves to go sit alone.

"Do you think either of those is my one true love?" Jason asked.

"I think you should either wait for fate to reveal her hand or try manifesting." I pretended to go into a trance.

"Want another pint?" Jason asked.

"Fuck me, this manifesting shit really does work, because that's exactly what I just had in my mind." I winked.

Jason bopped the top of my head as he walked past and towards the bistro.

CHAPTER FIVE

Merrin

Going out for a drink with my friend last night had been just what I'd needed. It had blown off the cobwebs so to speak, and this morning it was time to metaphorically blow off a few more. I had a quick shower and set off into Gnarly feeling full of purpose and vigour. First stop: *Seconds the Best*.

The bell tinkled as I walked in and a blonde and a brunette did a stereophonic groan while clutching their heads.

"That bad?" I asked.

Tilly, the brunette, nodded slowly. "I'm trying not to move."

Milly's hand was over her mouth. "And I'm trying not to be sick."

"Have you had some painkillers and water?" I asked them.

"Yes," Tilly said, this time not moving her head. "I could really use a coffee, but I'm—"

"Trying not to move." I finished off her sentence for her.

"It's usually Milly finishes my sentences." She tried to laugh, but then groaned again.

"I'll be back with coffee. For now, shall we close the shop back up?" I suggested.

"You're a superstar," Tilly said. She looked at Milly. "I'm not sure Milly can manage one but get two anyway. I can always drink hers as well. Take some money from the till."

"It's on me," I told them, and with that I walked out of the store, swinging the sign back to 'closed' on my way out, hearing another groan at the sound of the tinkling bell.

I had the perfect excuse now to go into Buns and Books. Entering the shop, I joined the queue and took a look at the gorgeous baking done by Callie who had been brought up as a tooth fairy. The sweet, sugary smells were a delight to my senses. I'd not woken hungover, but I had woken up hungry, and the quick slice of toast I'd eaten had done nothing to fill me up. Contrary to the myths about my kind, we did not feast on human flesh, but rather, the same food we'd eaten when human.

"Hey there, Merrin. What can I get you?" Callie said as I reached the front of the queue.

"Can I get two extra-strong coffees for the twins please to start?"

"Oh dear. That's not like them. What have they been up to?"

"A night on the town last night. Well, at the bistro. I just went to talk to them about some business and they can barely move."

Callie laughed. "It's good to see them getting out more and learning about life as two twenty-some-things, rather than staying cooped up in the shop and at home." She went and made their coffees and put them in a take-out bag with milk and sugar. "Tell them they're on the house."

"That's kind but it's okay, I said I'd treat them," I told her.

"Well, one good turn deserves another, Merrin, and so if you're buying their coffees, I'll buy yours. What are you having?"

By the time I'd finished I had three coffees, three

muffins, and three toasties, and only had to pay for the twins' order.

And the best thing was, even though I knew *she'd* be there, in the bookstore side, I never acknowledged her existence. Never looked her way. Gave Ginny no chance whatsoever to spoil the good mood I'd woken up in.

"Have a lovely day," I said to Callie, feeling satisfied with my morning so far, then I left the coffee shop and went back to the twins.

"You look a little better," I acknowledged Milly's pallor was less green.

"Let's just say I've made some room for coffee... but please, no food, not yet." She groaned. Her sister, however, leapt on the toastie like a dog facing a plate of freshly cooked sausages with no human in sight.

After enjoying the refreshments, it was down to business.

"After my accident, I've realised that the amount of furniture coming to my yard is just too much. We need to think of something else, because while I can recycle and repurpose things, even with Alistair taking some, I can't clear it fast enough."

The twins looked glum as they stared around their shop which was also full to bursting. "Everywhere is getting the same. People are forgetting to re-use stuff. They need a reminder," Tilly said.

"Hey!" Milly exclaimed. "Why don't you run some workshops?"

"What do you mean?" I asked, although an idea was already beginning to bloom in my mind.

"Get the people of Gnarly to book a workshop place for a price that covers the cost of materials and your time, and then they choose a piece of furniture and make it their own. After the workshop they take it with them or have it sent through the portal delivery system. You get to show off your talents with teaching them, the furniture gets re-purposed. It's a win-win."

"Why did I not think of that before?" I said out loud, while wondering why indeed I'd not thought of that before. It would also bring people near to my studio, where they could browse my craft pieces, rather than me only selling online, and might generate more income for me.

"So, to get this started, what would you need? Flyers with your telephone number and email on so people can contact you to book a place? Your materials? The place would need to be safe though." Milly pointed out. "Can't have your art students getting buried under furniture."

"Yeah, I'm going to tidy the place up. Haven't quite worked out how yet, but I can always pray for a miracle."

"If you could afford it, you should book the Letwine vampire builders to come modernise that cowshed. Look at how quickly they sorted Books and Buns," Milly suggested. "Though I'm guessing if you could have done it, you would have by now."

"No, actually, it's just been me being, well, zombie-like. Being slow and among decay. I'm realising after my claustrophobic breakdown experience that I can return to my zombie nature once I can chill out around a safe environment. That's why I need your help to make sure I get this stuff done.

"We're more than happy to help," they said in stereo, and then they laughed.

"It's weird when we do that now because it doesn't happen very often anymore," Milly explained.

Tilly got a pad and pen. "Okay, so you can also book Callie to provide refreshments and have breaks during the day. I'm guessing it would take a while. Let's set up a rough schedule of what a 'Design Day with Merrin' would be like.

We spent the next hour plotting out the workshop while consuming the rest of Callie's goods.

"That's perfect," I said honestly as I stared at the sheet of A4 paper in my hand. All I had to do now was to get my land set up and the workshops started. "I wonder if you could also help me with something else...?"

After leaving the shop, I not only had the workshop plan, but a couple of bags of clothes in my hands. Next on my agenda was an appointment to see Charity at *A Cut Above*. Charity had moved to Gnarly a month ago after being accepted by the council and had taken over what used to be a DVD hire store. Gnarly's residents had gone to London for their hair maintenance prior to this, so it was all very new and exciting for the residents to have their own salon.

When the twins had explained to her about my 'makeover', Charity had not only squeezed me in, but agreed to cut my hair in her kitchen and not in the salon.

As I approached the hairdressers, I went around the back as she'd directed.

"Come in," Charity called. She was a slim and

very pretty redhead. Her hair was scarlet and her eyes an emerald green.

"Mermaid," she said. "But call me Ariel and I'll feed you to the sharks."

I laughed and she laughed back.

"Sorry if I've caused inconvenience by not going in the salon."

"No, I get it. It's a huge change and can be overwhelming. Best we do it away from the eyes of the others, given that some of Gnarly love gossip more than they love their partners. It's for you to show off your new look, not for them to go telling everyone beforehand."

My heart thudded in my chest then. I'd never thought that I'd be gossip fodder for Gnarly just by getting a haircut. Plus, I'd be wearing clothes that fit. Surely this wasn't anything to get excited about?

Gnarly gets excited if someone clears their constipation, I thought. Being a small village, everyone was always up in your business the first chance they got. People would wonder why the sudden change in the local reclusive weirdo.

Well, I'd tell them the truth. My near-death-if-I-wasn't-already-dead experience had pressed the reset button on my undead life.

That's not the truth. You're doing it in some 'fuck

you' gesture to Ginny, my inner thoughts chided. Thank goodness I had wards from anyone reading my thoughts. Especially the bloody vampire herself.

"Okay, take a seat and let's do this," Charity said. "My next appointment is in thirty minutes, so we've plenty of time. Meanwhile, I've got a break from listening to my brother moaning about the terrible date he had last night."

"Oh dear. The curse of Gnarly has lifted but it doesn't mean our dating lives are any smoother, does it?"

"Not at all. So, what are we doing here?"

"Wh-what?" *Did she mean us? Was she propositioning me?*

Charity pointed at my head. "What style do you want?"

"Oh. Erm, I'll take your advice, but I was thinking..."

"Short? And let's trim that beard too. Get you a bit of a Christian Bale look going on."

"Yes," I agreed. I had no idea what I was going to end up looking like. I'd not been all emo-style only due to being a zombie. My parents had been hippies who'd lived off the land, having watched too many episodes of *The Good Life* together when they'd first met. I'd never had short hair. *Ever.*

Now in a salon you had a mirror to face. One that meant as you slowly transformed you saw it happen. But here in Charity's kitchen I did not. So all I had seen were large pieces of hair fall to the floor. I'd felt the draft on my neck where there'd been none before, and the cold metal of the scissors against my nape. Then the buzz of the razor as it shaved in layers.

Finally finished, with my beard trimmed too, Charity brushed the excess hair off my shoulders and removed my gown.

"Excuse my language, Merrin, but holy fucking hell. No one is going to recognise you. Your own mother wouldn't. Listen, I'm going to get the mirror. While I do, why not put on one of your new outfits?" While we'd been chatting as she'd cut my hair, I'd told her about my new clothes and general new image. She left the room.

As I stood there, part of me wanted to run back to my house. To the place where I just meandered around alone and did my own thing, because I had a feeling that I'd just started something akin to the beat of a butterfly's wing: created a ripple that would affect my life much beyond having no need any more for hair elastics. But I rummaged through the bags as yes, it was time to completely let go of the old me and welcome the new one.

Charity returned carrying a full-length mirror, with the mirror part facing her.

"Jesus. Brace yourself," she said. She had the mirror covered with an old curtain and placed it in front of me.

"I feel like I'm on a TV show." I laughed.

But that laugh turned to utter silence when she removed the curtain and I saw my reflection. Short brown hair styled with a little product and off my face, and a smart beard. No longer could I hide behind my hair. I was wearing jeans that fit my actual shape and a pale blue t-shirt with a camel-coloured short-sleeved jacket. While I'd never be anything but slim, I didn't look emaciated. I looked healthy, fit almost. I was just a bit pale.

"Can I do something?" Charity said, pointing to my face.

I nodded because I was too stunned to speak.

She got a tube from her pocket and after removing the lid, she pushed a little into the palm of her hand. She got me to lower my face and dotted it on my complexion and into my neck, then rubbed it in.

"Now look."

Gone were the milk-bottle tones of my skin. A healthy glow matched my complexion to my newly shorn hair and beard.

"Here." She gave it to me. "You might want to look into an all over fake-tan."

"Thank you, Charity. I—"

"You're overwhelmed. It's not the first time I've done a complete makeover and this has happened. But it doesn't happen very often, and it's been my absolute pleasure to do it. Are you happy? Just nod your head, so I don't worry you think you've made the biggest mistake ever and I've got it all wrong."

I nodded.

"You just take your time and get used to your new look while I get my kitchen swept up. Do you want a hot drink or anything?"

"No, thank you. Gosh, I look so different. I'm feeling a bit nervous of going back 'out there'."

She gave me a sympathetic smile. "People are definitely going to stare, Merrin, so prepare yourself. You look entirely different and it's going to have Gnarly gossiping. I can imagine them all now. 'Did you see Merrin? Do you reckon the furniture banged him hard on the head? Done him a favour though, hasn't it?'" Charity impersonated one of the gossipiest old ladies, Barb, perfectly. It was something I was good at doing, impersonating other people's voices, but I didn't tell her that. It did make me get brave though.

"Listen, do you want to come out for a drink some-time? You know, to get to know Gnarly a bit better?"

"Like on a date or just as an introduction to the village?"

"Well... a date, or you could ask your brother too and it could just be a general drink."

"I'd like that, Merrin, and I'll not ask my brother."

Did she mean she would go out with me on a date then? As I stood feeling even more displaced than before, she grabbed a small business card.

"My mobile number is on there. How about you get used to your new appearance and then if you still want to grab that drink with me, you give me a call?"

I nodded and then after paying her for my haircut, I left.

CHAPTER SIX

Ginny

I was at the shop bright and early the next day, and while I didn't get any nutrition from drinking coffee and eating pastries, it was a bonus that every day would start with them.

The smells in the shop were incredible. It was a time where having my vampire super-smelling abilities was a bonus. Baked goods, coffee, hot chocolate, and my new favourite thing... the smell of books. I'd told Lawrie I was annoyed at the fact he was lovesick and worked amongst pink, but now I was beginning to understand. The shop was how you'd imagine heaven to be; somewhere Lawrie and I had been denied by the events of our deaths.

I'd enjoyed lazing around last night and reading.

Knowing that unless something horrendous befell me, I would live for eternity, had got me all 'butterflies fluttering in my stomach' excited as I thought about how many books there were in the world for me to read. I didn't have to suffer what customers were telling me: how they wanted to read one more chapter before going to sleep, but their eyes closed and despite their best efforts, the next day they couldn't remember the last few pages. No, I only needed the smallest amount of sleep, just an hour, and then I could carry on. I needed to buy a few more books today. I'd have no wages left at this rate.

Many vampires were rich because they'd lived a long time and had invested in property or businesses back in the day. They'd had time to learn several different career paths, or they'd enthralled and cheated wealthy humans.

I was relatively new in terms of vampire years, having been turned in the seventies, and I had yet to acquire any skills that would set me off on a path to riches.

Pulling myself back into the present moment, I watched as Merrin walked in. My guard up, I waited for him to fix me with a look of distaste, or to walk over to insult me. But he didn't. He didn't look over to where I was *at all*. He got served, said bye to Callie, and then left the store.

The ungrateful motherfucker.

Had I not saved him from a pile of rubble yesterday? From the torment of having to wait a claustrophobic's eternity to be rescued? I'd saved him a therapy bill and yet he didn't even have the common decency to insult me.

And that was the moment I realised I had issues. Because I liked the fact I got into sparring wars with Merrin.

I loved to hate him.

He provided an outlet to all my frustrations, and the fact he didn't seem to care that I insulted him and gave back as good as he got meant I'd actually found something to do that didn't become boring in five seconds flat.

My new daily activities had become: work in the store, annoy Merrin, read books, and now today he'd not given me the satisfaction of tearing him down.

That wouldn't do at all.

"Virginia. How goes it? I hope you're not slipping your number out along with the purchases to anyone who seems to have a spare few pounds." Lawrie had entered the store and after kissing his wife had come over to me.

"I'm behaving, because..." I lowered my voice. "I really like this job, Lawrie. It's so much nicer than the stupid Vampire's In(n). No one leering at me, or being rude, or spilling drinks. Customers here know that if they get food or drink on the books they have to purchase them. It's an entirely different atmosphere."

Lawrie stood for a moment, looked me up and down, and then felt at my forehead, despite the fact vampires did not have human ailments that caused temperatures.

"Have you been bewitched? Only, a couple of days ago, you said you hated everyone being happy and now... you look dangerously close to being exactly that yourself. You'll be falling in love next."

"Huh. I think not. Falling for a rich man's wallet, yes. Falling in love, no."

Lawrie looked down at me with a frown. "You really need to get over this, Ginny. It was a long time ago. You don't need tons of money."

Lawrie hinting at my past made my eyes hurt, so I knew they'd just flashed red. I fought to keep my temper and my teeth under control. My incisors were threatening to come down.

"If he wasn't already dead and dusted, I'd kill him..." I spat out.

Lawrie walked around the back of my counter and folded me into his arms. "But he is, and at least we are free of our sire. Who knows what life would have been like if William had not been dealt with by the breedents?"

I nodded into his chest. Then I pushed him away. "You've got so soft since you got married, I barely recognise you."

"Callie said you helped Merrin yesterday..."

I pulled a face.

"She did point out that you did it as a sign of power and hostility, so at least I knew you'd not suddenly had a complete personality transplant."

"I detest that individual. My actions were entirely self-satisfying."

Lawrie smirked at me. God, at times he could be insufferable. "What?"

"I'm just thinking about how Callie and I loved to hate each other and look at us now." With that he shot out of my range and appeared back at his wife's side before I could launch the corner of a book at his eye.

While I carried on serving customers, I started to think about what Aria and I had talked about last night. About moving to Gnarly. It would be amazing, but at the moment it was nothing more than a dream for me. I couldn't afford it. That didn't stop me trying to find a way to make claim to some land though. Aria and Bernard could get their home built and I could get my plans approved for the future, or Aria and Bernard could build both and I could rent from them.

Always the poor one who has to beg, I thought, and my mind whirled back to a time long before.

"What's for tea?" my brother Duncan asked as he walked in from school. It was only four pm, but four-teen-year-old boys had appetites as big as my mum's debts—huge.

I gave him a bread and jam sandwich.

"Oh, not this again. I had it for lunch," he complained. I didn't tell him that it was my lunch he'd just eaten, that I'd gone without in order that he could eat.

"It's all we have. Sorry."

*Duncan huffed but feasted on the sandwich. Wiping the back of his hand across his mouth he said, "Okay, I'm still **starving**, so what else is there?"*

The truth? There was nothing else. Not one damn thing left in the house. Our mum had fallen apart when our father had left her for another woman and she'd slid into a mess of drink and drugs. When she wasn't uncon-

scious, she was stealing to buy more of both. She'd forgotten we existed, or rather she'd told me that as an eighteen-year-old, I could now stop sponging and provide for the household.

I was a student, learning sciences, and hoping one day to become a vet. I loved animals. Mum's debts had meant me having to give up our six-year-old cocker spaniel, Marla, for adoption as I could no longer afford to feed her. It had broken my heart, so much so that I didn't think it would ever repair. It hurt far more than the pangs of hunger that was for sure. Now it looked like I was going to have to give up my studies too and get a job. I already worked on a weekend and a few evenings, but that didn't go far into buying food for us. I needed a full-time job to do when Duncan was at school, so that I could be around for him when he was home. Not that he did much more than lounge in his room listening to music, gaming, or hanging with his mates.

But we couldn't carry on like this. What was next? Not being able to make rent? Losing our home? I'd taken a wild guess at how our mum was managing to pay for it so far, and it filled me with horror. I somehow needed to get help for mum too, before I came home to find her dead.

"You do your homework and I'll go do a food shop," I instructed Duncan. Grabbing my coat, I told him I'd be back soon, and I set off for the corner shop. I'd rummage in the bins around the back and hope for the best.

I was almost there, and in a daydream wondering about how I could change our fortunes. The street was busy, and people bustled about, mums calling in to do their shopping after collecting their kids from school. Ours had used to be one of those mums.

"Sorry, sorry," a man said as he smacked into me. I turned and saw him scold a young child for distracting him from looking where he was going. Seeing a small black rectangle on the floor, I bent down to pick it up. The man had dropped his wallet as we'd collided. I was about to call him back when I halted. Instead, I quickly looked around to see if anyone was watching me and when I saw they weren't, I darted into a shop doorway. Rifling through the wallet, I found it had six pounds in it. My heart leaped with excitement. Tonight we could eat. Guilt quickly passed through me and away, as I decided to take it as a sign of fate that this had happened. That way it was easier to not acknowledge my theft.

I headed into the shop where I bought bread, sandwich meats, potatoes and vegetables, and some spam. I *even treated Duncan to some crisps and chocolate and a small bottle of pop.*

That night, watching his face light up as he crammed the food in his mouth, and seeing him look so content when he'd finished, I vowed that we'd be hungry no longer.

Instead of getting a job, I'd 'bump into' more people on the street. That way I could continue my studies yet keep our bellies full and a roof over our heads.

"Do you have any books on home decorating?" A female voice brought me away from the past, and I looked at the redhead in front of me.

"Only a couple at present, but I can order anything else into store," I told her. "Let me show you what we have." Glad from the reprieve from my thoughts, I smiled at the woman.

I pulled the two books from the shelf. "Feel free to grab a coffee and peruse, but know that spills mean purchases," I informed her, holding out the books.

She took them from me and quickly flicked through. "I'll take both please, and then I'll do exactly that. Only, I've not much time before my next appointment, so it's a quick toastie and back to it I go. Then when I've finished, I need to try to make a start on the apartment because it's in dire need."

I nodded. "Okay, let's get you sorted then, so you can enjoy your lunch."

"I'm Charity, the new hairdresser in town," she said. "Let me know if you need a re-style."

"Ginny. Vampire. Stuck with what I've got," I explained.

Charity nodded. "I'm available for updos for special occasions, blow-dries, etc. Doesn't have to be a complete makeover." Her cheeks turned pink. "Sorry, I'm not meaning to come across like I'm touting hard for business. I'm just a bit hyper. I did an amazing restyle for a customer, and it's left me buzzing."

"Before I got this job, I wouldn't have understood that," I replied honestly. "But I love working here and I'm buzzing that I just sold two books. Are you doing a restyle on your place too?"

She nodded. "It needs it. Although my younger brother can be a pain in the arse and will probably pooh-pooh all my ideas."

Immediately I thought of Duncan again, and swallowed hard, trying to push him back out of my mind.

"Feed him first. That usually works," I said.

"Good idea, I'll try that," she replied. I swiped her credit card, bagged up her books and she gave me a little wave goodbye. "Good to meet you, Ginny," she said.

She seemed a really nice person. Genuine. Someone I would have liked to have as a friend. But I couldn't hear her talk about her brother. It would hurt too much. I busied myself ordering two different home decorating books for the store until the moment of pain had been forgotten, buried deep down once more.

CHAPTER SEVEN

Merrin

I'd spent much of the evening gazing at my reflection in the mirror. Not because I was vain, but because I couldn't actually believe that the person looking back at me was *me*. I looked *that* different.

I woke up with renewed vigour, ready to make a start on my plot of land. I made myself some breakfast, some strong coffee to set me up for the morning, and then getting changed into some old jeans and a t-shirt, I took myself out to the cowshed.

Somehow, I had to make a space here for people to work in. My studio didn't have enough room for people to work on large items of furniture. Maybe Milly was right, and I needed to get the Letwine vampires out here? They could make me a large practical workshop. I could extend the studio. I needed to get in touch with their architect, get some plans drawn up and then submit them to the council. That meant I either needed to talk to Mya, Lawrie, or dare I say it, Ginny, to get in touch with the Letwine architect for me. I wasn't sure which was worst. The sassy vampire who stuck her nose in and usually caused disaster; the sarcastic vampire who had only ever really been interested in himself other than his sister, and now his wife; or that sister who was a pain in the arse. Putting it out of my mind for now, I was just about to do some preparation work on Fenella's bureau when I realised she might want to work on it herself as part of my workshop.

I began to feel irritated. Just a general feeling like you got if you'd not had enough sleep and every little thing that didn't go right started to feel like a major nuisance. Clearly, I needed to go into Gnarly. I'd ring ahead to see if I could meet Fenella and then I'd consider who to ask to put me in touch with the architect.

But firstly, I needed to get changed into something a little smarter and make sure I looked tidy, because it was the first time people would see the new 'me'.

"I don't know how you got into Gnarly or what you're selling, but I suggest you clear off, before I get my man on you and he's a big, strong brute who will throw you off my land," Fenella shouted through the letterbox.

"Santa is more likely to give me a cuddle, Fen, and you know it," I shouted back through.

There was silence for a moment and then the door flew open.

Fenella peered at me closely, up and down, like she was an X-ray machine at an airport.

"Merrin? Is that you?"

"It is. I've had a bit of a restyle. Can I come in then or do you need my fingerprints?"

She stood back to let me in. "Merrin, I'm flummoxed. You look so different. I didn't recognise you."

"Yeah, I guessed that when you threatened me with your rugged boyfriend, Father Christmas." I laughed.

"He's just started going back to the gym actually," she whispered conspiratorially. "He's put a few pounds on since we started dating. With Christmas in six months' time, he can't afford to let his health slide."

I was sure Santa was getting some stamina training

with Fenella, but I wasn't about to say that to my friend's mum.

"Come and sit down and I'll get you a drink and a slice of cake. Is coffee and a slice of carrot cake, okay?"

"Sounds fantastic, Fen. Thank you."

She bustled around the kitchen clattering mugs and saucers and boiling the kettle, and before long we were sat at her kitchen table with hot beverages and the most gorgeous smelling cake.

"Right. Tell me more about this workshop and how I can help."

I showed Fenella the plans the twins had helped me draw up. Fenella had always been the main organiser of events in Gnarly Fell and so her input would be priceless.

"So if you have time could you help me? You can have your bureau free of charge."

"I would love to help you and no payment is necessary. If it's okay with you, can I supervise, and you do my bureau? You could show people the techniques. Only I'm great at arranging but I'm not great at anything practical beyond baking. I have an eye for what looks good, but I would ruin the piece. I want to pay you for your work, Merrin. You work hard."

"You should get something for your assistance," I argued.

"I will. I'll get to spend my day with other villagers enjoying myself. I'm in my element making sure everyone is fed and watered and so you leave that to me."

That was good. I didn't need the cupcake café to help with refreshments then. Fen had it all handled.

"So what timescale were you thinking?"

I told Fenella about how I needed to tidy up my land.

"I either need to get the vampires on it quickly, or I make do for now, seeing as plans need drawing up and submitting for approval."

"We're forecast to have great weather for the rest of the month, so why don't we set up the first workshop for Sunday?"

"This Sunday?" My mouth dropped open. It was Wednesday now. Could I get things ready to have a first workshop in four days?

"Yes. What's there to do other than get some flyers up and word of mouth and get prepared?" Fen was full of enthusiasm. "The sooner you start, the sooner you get your place cleared up. People can work in the cowshed. Just ask that vampire woman who rescued you from the furniture avalanche if she can help you again. She'd get it moved in no time. Maybe she could bring the architect with her too?"

"You heard about my accident then?"

Fen tipped her head to one side and fixed me with a smirk. "Merrin, this is Gnarly. We all know about your accident. Plus, my son is one of the biggest gossips of them all."

"Jason told you all about it then?"

"He did. He also mentioned something interesting about your rescuer. I gather you don't get along?" Fen arched a brow.

I felt my nostrils flare. "That's an understatement. So you can see my difficulty in asking for her help again."

"Nonsense, Merrin. We all have to get along. She works here in the fell now, so you must do your best to make amends. You don't have to like her, or become her new best friend, but you must ask her to the workshop. Oh and ask Charity and her brother too, with them being our latest arrivals."

I smiled as she said that. Fenella's eyes narrowed in on me. "Oooh, of course. I'm guessing Charity cut your hair. You like her then?"

"She seems a lovely person."

"Hmm, definitely get her to the workshop. And you must make Jason go. Maybe he might meet someone there. What about this Ginny girl?"

I snorted.

"Not unless he has a few million hidden under his mattress." I told her about Ginny's materialistic ways.

"Hmm, I shall keep an eye on that one then. Callie speaks highly of her though, and she seemed nice enough to me when I popped into the shop yesterday."

"Well, I can only go on what side of her she's shown me, and it's not been pretty."

With that Fen changed the conversation onto a hearty plotting of what needed to be done. She opened her laptop and designed a gorgeous flyer with ease, clearly practiced in such things, and then she handed one to me. It said the date, cost, time, and what they'd need to bring with them, with food and refreshments provided.

"I'll go take the rest of these around the shops and the community centre. They've got your email on so look out for replies, so we know how many to expect. We'll set a limit at twelve, plus us two."

"Thanks, Fen. Are you sure you don't want me to go hand out the flyers?"

"You just take that one to Books and Buns," she said. "And go make nice with the vampire woman because we need her help."

My face must have given away my feelings on the subject because Fenella placed a hand on my arm.

"If there's one thing I've learned from my time

here in Gnarly, Merrin, it's that everyone has a story, and I'm sure Ginny is no different. If she feels superior while she's helping you, let her. Inside, you know you're the one winning, not having to enlist professionals to help you move the furniture."

I nodded, and it got me thinking. Why was Ginny like that? So mercenary and cruel. Was it because she was an evil vampire, or was it because of something else? My past had shaped me. Maybe Ginny's had shaped her.

I made a decision that I would go ask for her help and be polite. I mean hadn't my parents brought me up that way?

Just because she reminded me of the bad things in my past, didn't mean I had to drag it into my future.

I hugged Fen, said goodbye, and made my way to Books and Buns, flyer in hand, and resolve in my soul.

I kept saying hello to people and they kept ignoring me. I found it entirely peculiar until I walked into the café and Dela squinted her eyes at me. "You look familiar," she said. "Are you related to someone from the fell?"

"It's me, Merrin," I said, my voice lowered, and I

watched as her eyes went wide. Her hand went over her mouth. "Oh my god, you look amazing, and so, so different." I noted her eyes flip to the other side of the store, to the bookshop.

I held out my flyer. "I was wondering if you could put this in the window for me?" Dela looked it over. "Oh, this looks like fun. Count me in. I want some storage for my guest room, and oh, put my mum down for a place too. She can make something for her cabin."

Dela and Callie's mum, Sheridan, had moved to Gnarly in the new year. The council had allowed a small log cabin to be built close to Dela's new home on the same piece of land that the trees didn't grow on any longer, due to a previous fungal infestation that had thankfully been thwarted in its tracks before it took out any more trees.

"Great. That's two already. We're thinking maybe a dozen people altogether."

"Sounds good. I'll ask Callie later, and Chantelle. I don't suppose Ginny's invited...?"

"Actually, I need to go talk to her about something. Try to make some kind of a truce."

"Really? Oh, this I need to see. Hold on while I get Lawrie out here so I can come and tidy the tables nearby."

"Don't even try to hide your amusement at my

predicament, Dela. It's fine. I'll just die while I have to try to play nice with the evil vampire because I need her help," I said with a good dose of heavy sarcasm.

Dela shook her head. "That's not why I'm coming over to nosy, Merrin."

"No?" I felt my brow crease.

"Merrin, you're unrecognisable, and, excuse my language, but you look hot as fuck. I want to be looking at her face when she realises who you are."

"Oh!" I exclaimed.

I looked 'hot as fuck?'

This makeover was going to take some getting used to. It looked like Merrin Bruckman couldn't hide away anymore if he wanted to.

Taking a deep breath, I made my way over to the bookstore side, but then I chickened out and went to pick up a book instead. I found myself staring at a copy of 'Investing in Success', a book for successful businessmen.

I felt a presence come to my side. Hah! The stuck-up vamp bitch thought I was a potential rich victim. I'd show her.

I whizzed around.

To find I was being sniffed.

Ginny stood away from me, hands on her hips. She was clearly concentrating, her face scrunched, eyes closed.

Finally, she opened her eyes and looked at me. "I didn't think it could be possible. Thought it must be a sibling. There's a different note there. You changed your shower gel?"

"Are you smelling me?"

"I can smell everyone without having to be that close to them," Ginny retorted. "Superior sense of smell, remember? But you usually smell of fusty cowshed. Today you smell of citrus and sandalwood, and coconut hair products. I came closer to double check and see if it really was you, and you were, in fact, capable of bathing, or if you were a relation."

"Jesus, Ginny," Dela huffed out. "I made my way over here to see your reaction to Merrin's new look and you knew it was him because you could smell him?"

"Well, duh," Ginny replied. "Vampire."

Dela moved back to the cupcake counter, failing to hide her disappointment as she shook her head.

"So what do you want?" Ginny said in a surly tone. "Because I know it's not that book. That's for successful minted businessmen, not losers."

It took all of my inner strength to not put my hands

around her neck. That, and knowing that she could bat me off like a midge.

"I need your help please, Ginny," I said.

That did it. Her face took on an overall appearance of shock, exactly what Dela had hoped to see when Ginny had noted my new look. No, that wasn't what had knocked Ginny off her pedestal.

It was her enemy suddenly being nice.

On the outside, I kept my polite expression, but inwardly I smirked with complete and utter satisfaction as I remembered what my mum used to say to me: 'Kill your enemies with kindness, Merrin. It hurts them more'.

Oh, I was about to become the kindest, nicest person ever.

CHAPTER EIGHT

Ginny

I was glad vampires had a superior sense of smell. That, and the fact that Merrin had stayed at the counter for a time while he asked Dela to place him a flyer in the window. He'd forgotten my super-hearing too. Though I couldn't make out his conversation, I could make out it was him. It gave me time to prepare, because as soon as I'd heard his voice and tried to work out how Merrin's vocal chords were coming out of the smart man at the counter, and then realising Merrin *was* the smart man at the counter; well, I'd needed a moment to deal with my shock.

As he'd walked over, I'd pretended to be busy with the till, and then I'd looked up to find Merrin had picked a book up, Dela nearby. What was going on? As Dela looked over to me, with a smirk on her face, I realised. She thought I was going to be fooled by his new appearance.

No, not fooled. I was taken aback though as Merrin turned to face me.

He looked good. Really good. There was no denying it. The unwashed, skinny, tall zombie had been visited by some fairy godmother and turned into a prince. I wasn't blind. Despite the fact I hated him, he now looked and smelled good on the outside. It didn't make the inside any better though. Or so I thought until he...

Asked me for my help. Politely.

I needed a lie down. Gnarly had always been a bizarre place with strange happenings. Callie and Dela had told me a lot of tales, but this... Merrin mark two. I needed a moment to process.

I went with the word that was stuck in my throat. "Pardon?"

"I wanted to ask for your help with a project. Erm, if it's not convenient here, could you tell me a time and place that is?"

"What project?" I needed to know if this was all an elaborate trick designed to make me look foolish.

"I'm running an upcycling workshop at my place on Sunday. It's to help clear some of the furniture away and to encourage re-purposing and re-using.

Only, I need to get the cowshed sorted quickly, and well, after the other day…" He paused. "I thought I'd ask you."

My first thought was to tell him to go fuck himself, but then I remembered Aria and my plan to put houses on his land. I had to tread carefully though. He'd get suspicious if I wasn't a pain in his backside.

"Why would I help you again? You're a jerk."

I saw Merrin swallow. He might be acting nice, but his movements gave him away. He was wishing he had a stake right now.

"Don't think of it as helping me. Think of it as helping Gnarly. After all, the people here are being welcoming to you."

I made him wait a little longer before agreeing. "Fine. I'll come over to your place after work. I'll be there around six."

With that I walked off and went back to my counter and refused to look at him again. I heard him walk away and say goodbye to Dela.

It was then I noticed there was a twenty-pound note on the table next to the bookshelf. I wandered over and saw he'd taken the book. Huh, looked like Merrin had ideas above his station. It'd take more than a few upcycles to make him a decent amount of money. Selling his land, now that was a more realistic option for him.

The moment the place had a lull in business, Dela came over to my side. "So, what did you think? Still hate him?"

I sighed and rolled my eyes. "If someone shaved a skunk, would it not still stink?"

"What did he want to talk to you about? He said he wanted to make some kind of truce."

I scoffed. "He doesn't want a truce. He just wants use of my super-strength. The puny weakling needs help moving his furniture and so he came slithering in to ask me to help him."

I actually felt a bit mean as I said this as the guy had asked me politely.

"I'm guessing you told him where to go then. Shame. I'm looking forward to the workshop."

"No, I said I'd help," I replied.

Dela stared at me with focus. "What?"

"I said I'd help."

"Did he offer you money?"

I guffawed. "Of course, the man formerly known as a hobo offered me money. Don't be silly. He just basically begged for my help, so I said yes. It's an opportunity to watch him squirm and also feel weak and inferior at the side of me."

Dela leant on the table near me.

"Is that really your aim? Do you dislike him that much?" She paused. "It's what he said to you that day, isn't it? How he shamed you for wanting a man with money. That really did hit a major nerve."

I looked at the floor.

"Why does his opinion matter so much, Ginny? You do you. And if that's marry a man for money, not love, then go for it. Don't let grumpy Merrin's judgement swamp your shoulders. And certainly don't let it eat you up so much that all you can think about is hurting him back. Just be indifferent."

My friend sounded like she was speaking from experience, and I guessed I knew the root cause of this.

"Are you thinking about your dad?"

Dela nodded. "My father doesn't want to get to know Callie or myself because he wants to keep the Royal Court trouble free and not bring shame upon his wife. And I totally understand that; I do. The cost would be huge, and the queen has already helped us enough. But at first, I hated him. What father doesn't want to know his daughters? Now, though, I have a good relationship with my mother, a loving husband of my own, and I've realised that I'm not missing a father who I've never had. I was making up a dream person, someone I imagined would be overawed to see me. I was craving acceptance and Nick pointed out the truth; all I needed to do was to accept myself."

I thought about what Nick had told her.

You just need to accept yourself. I murmured the affirmation in my mind.

"Merrin's words hurt because something in them must have rung true. You need to look deep into yourself at why, and then accept who you are or make changes if needed." Dela took a breath. "Jesus, I'm spending too much time around Mya. I sound like a self-help guru. Sorry, Ginny. I didn't mean to come over and start a lecture."

"No, Dela, you're absolutely right," I replied. "The things Merrin said cut deep and I need to look into why that is."

I needed to take a good hard look at myself and decide what I wanted, and what I needed.

And I might have to ask Mya for some guidance.

But for now, I needed to finish work and then make my way over to the farm.

I whizzed to the perimeter of the land where rickety fence panels surrounded what must be over an acre of land. It was more or less level, and wildflowers and shrubs grew in between the rotted and broken panels. At the other side was Gnarly woodland, with the gnarled branched trees that gave the fell its name. I walked up the driveway, a mixture of sand, clay, and stones, and assessed the plot as I went. There was scrap and furniture everywhere, some covered in waterproof tarpaulin, some exposed to the weather. I saw old metal gates, chimney pots, piles of broken up wood. It was just one huge mess.

As I reached the top of the land, the cowshed came close to view, along with Merrin's home and his studio. If the land was cleared there would be plenty of room for Merrin and he could easily allow two more homes to be built near him. Aria and Bernard would make it worth his while. He could split the land and the other houses be placed near the bottom. Aria would love looking out over the woodland. I wondered if any supes lived out there. When I called Mya, I'd ask her.

As I walked past the cowshed, I realised that Merrin had not told me where to meet him. Walking towards his front door, it opened and he walked outside, giving me a brief wave in acknowledgement.

As we met up there was a huge awkwardness as we

looked at the other, neither of us knowing what to say. We didn't do hello; we did why don't you fuck right off.

I cast my eyes over Merrin again. The truth was he really did scrub up well. He looked handsome. But appearances meant nothing to me. They were deceptive. I'd learned to trust no one. If you kept yourself acerbic and distant, you stayed away from danger. If you let no one in, they couldn't hurt you. Yes, it was better I served a large slice of what Merrin expected: Surliness, sarcasm, and sass.

"What's with the makeover of yourself and this shit tip?" I went for the jugular, but only rhetorically for a change.

"It's just time." He shrugged. "I couldn't carry on like this. Hiding away from life." As he spoke, he looked a little taken aback. "Shit," he said. "That's it. I've avoided life for years, thinking I was safer here, on my own land, and then when the furniture landed on me, it showed me that there's danger everywhere. That's at the root of all this. Refusing to hide away anymore because what's the point? If shit is going to hit the fan, it can happen anywhere."

"Erm, right," I said, more than a little discomforted by Merrin's honest admission. "So where do you need me to help?"

"The cowshed first. That needs clearing ready for the workshop. I know it's going to take time to get my land back from the salvage, the excess furniture, and from where Mother Nature has attempted to take it back, but for the first time in a long time I feel like I have aims. It's like I've suddenly woken up from a coma or something."

I felt weird for a moment and then I realised what it was. Concern. It had been a while since I'd felt that emotion. "Maybe something weird is going on with you and you should see a doctor? Like, aren't you supposed to walk around everywhere extra slow and wailing?" I asked him, as he was being super strange and not at all Merbin.

"And do you spook at the sight of garlic and need to avoid sunlight?" he snapped. Phew, the Merrin I knew was still there. Arsehole.

"No, though at least in the dark your face would be less conspicuous. And garlic, being pungent, would mask the smell of your body."

"At least if I wailed it would drown out the sound of your incessant bitching," he retorted.

And then the strangest thing happened. As each of us stared at the other, waiting for the next barbed insult, I began to laugh, and then Merrin joined in.

"As much as insulting you is the ultimate entertainment, I actually did come here to help you, so let's go see what needs doing," I said.

"Shall we call a temporary truce?" Merrin suggested. "It will get the task done quicker if we aren't bickering."

"Agreed." I held out my hand and he took mine in his and we shook. But as we did something weird happened. A tingle went right from my hand, and it seemed to fizz through my body.

We sprang apart. "Electric shock," Merrin said, as if what had transpired just then had been static electricity.

But as my lady parts woke from a deep slumber, I wasn't sure that's what it had been at all.

CHAPTER NINE

Merrin

What the hell had just happened? One minute we were laughing, the next she'd shaken my hand and some kind of zing had fired up my zang, if you caught my drift.

Seeing Ginny looking as uncomfortable as I did and guessing the strange electricity had shot through her too, I blamed static and started for the cowshed.

The last time we'd been here, Ginny had been picking furniture off me. This time we were on a more equal footing where I wasn't having an emotional claustrophobic breakdown and was thinking about my business instead.

"So, ideally, I need to go through these items and get them safely organised. I thought I'd take out the furniture that would make good, simple makeover pieces and put them over there," I said, pointing to one corner that was packed tight, "ready for Sunday. But as you can see, first I have to make some space in general."

"How about I do what they do on the cluttered house programmes, Merrin? I'll move absolutely everything outside and then you can tell me what to do with the furniture one thing at a time."

"Sounds good," I said. "Erm, why did you agree to help me again, only this all feels very weird."

"I can call you Merbin if it makes you feel any better?" she drawled.

"No thanks."

She placed her arms across her chest, making me notice she had small boobs. A nice amount to fit in a hand. I actually put my fist in my mouth, appalled at my thoughts.

We hate her. I reminded my libido. What had that shock thing done to me?

"Have you put a thrall on me? I have wards in place, but just checking?"

"Oh good lord, are you freaking out, Merbin because I'm not being a psycho?" She rolled her eyes hard. "Listen up. I like Gnarly Fell. It's much better than the Letwine mansion and I'd like to move here one day if I can. If I spend time getting involved with the community it will look good when I apply to live here. So that's why I'm helping. Nothing to do with you. It benefits Gnarly and mostly it benefits me, and we all know how much I love myself, right? You happy now?'

I nodded. "Yes, now I see that it's to further your own interests that's much more believable and therefore settles the discomfort that was rolling inside of me. You being genuinely nice didn't ring true."

She huffed. Stomped over to the corner that had been earmarked for the workshop furniture and with speed began moving everything outside.

I wondered if I'd gone too far. It wasn't like I knew the woman well. But I did know a poor unfortunate soul who'd once been out on a date with her: a fellow artist who lived in London. I'd sat with him one night when all he'd talked about was the vampire woman who'd led him a merry dance of chasing after her, only for him to be suckered in and find out it was clear she wanted his money and not love. Once Lawrie had come to the village and his sister visited, it soon became clear she was the Virginia my friend Rupert had talked about. Since then, his work had become dark and morose and he didn't come out anymore, preferring to stay in some kind of tormented fugue state. No woman should have the power to do that to a man. To ruin him. It reminded me of my own losses because of the power of a woman. Something I'd vowed would never happen again.

And this was the truth about why I'd been so dismissive of Ginny. By leading my friend into his dark ruin, she reminded me of what I myself had faced, and I didn't want a reminder. It was why I wanted her gone.

But now. Now she was working in Gnarly and talking about living here.

That meant I either had to get used to her and what she represented, or... I had to drive her out of here.

Before today, I'd have happily got behind the wheel, but as I watched Ginny looking pissed off in an upset way, rather than an 'I want to break all your bones' way, I wondered if it was possible that I'd misjudged her.

So give her a chance, Merrin, I heard my inner conscience tell me. Go ahead with the truce and see what she reveals. *Then if she's as selfish as you first thought, rid Gnarly of her presence by turning the villagers against her.*

It was a plan of sorts, and so I strode outside with purpose, determined to form some kind of a tentative friendship with the woman.

"I'm sorry. Genuinely. And look, you've not had to force the apology out of me this time," I said, as I moved closer to the salty vampire. I had to appreciate the fact that she was neither out of breath (helps if you didn't breathe), nor had broken a sweat. She was stretching out her limbs, which revealed a slight sliver of skin between the bottom of her t-shirt and the top of her jeans.

"I don't fucking care. Stick your opinions up your arse where shit belongs." She narrowed her gaze.

I stepped closer to her. "Whether you care or not, and I think you do because it's clearly demonstrated in your manner, I do heartily and genuinely apologise."

"Have you heard yourself, Merbin?" She impersonated my tone. "'Gincompoop, it's clearly demonstraaaattted in your mannnerrrrr'. You are such a condescending twat." She stomped her foot on the ground. "How do you manage to be so uppity when you've spent so much time under the ground?"

"I don't mean to be." I decided to be honest. "Look, I heard some things about you, that made me form an opinion of you without my knowing you personally. And you weren't exactly kind yourself, judging me on my appearance and how I live. Please, please, please, can we make a truce and actually try to get to know the other a little, because if you do intend to live here then it won't be good for the village if we hate each other."

I watched as her eyes flitted towards the bottom of the field and the woodland. "That's shifter territory," I said.

"Huh?" She gave me a blank look.

"The woods. The part that backs onto my land is shifter territory, although at the moment there aren't many shifters in Gnarly. Mainly Jason and then Mitzi from the general store. You'd not be allowed to live there."

"Oh, right. Thanks for the heads up," she replied.

"We're full at the moment. At present, other than Charity who applied to take over an empty business premises, Gnarly's residents have increased by the new relationships formed since the curse lifted. If a place becomes available, it's possible they'd consider your application. But because you can travel quickly due to your vamp speed and have a place in Chelsea, they wouldn't see it as a priority," I told her honestly.

"So unless I take over a business premise..."

"Of which there currently aren't any empty ones," I finished.

"Or I marry a resident?" she enquired.

I swallowed. My mouth and throat suddenly as dry as clothes left to bake too long on a washing line.

"Your face." She laughed. "Don't worry. I'm not going to marry Jason just so I can live in the woods. You already know I like the finer things in life. I currently have a very comfortable, well-furnished apartment. I'm also immortal, so I can happily put my name on a waiting list and for the years that pass to seem like no time at all to me. So, calm down before you make flyers warning all the men of Gnarly that I'm on a mission for a husband."

I remained speechless, because my mind *had* gone to her marrying my friend, and I'd worried that she'd do the same to bubbly Jason that she'd done to Rupert. I'd need to keep a close eye on Virginia Letwine because you couldn't trust the words of an evil vampire.

"Okay, what's next?" She pointed to the furniture.

"Next, can you help me with a few repairs to the cowshed? I meant to ask you to get me the details of the Letwine architect as I'd like to make a few changes to the place. That will have to wait for another day now."

"Okay."

Once we got back into the cowshed, Ginny proved herself very useful as she helped me to patch up some leaking parts of the roof. The fact she could fly up there made me quite jealous I'd not been turned, as opposed to the fate I'd ended up with.

While she did that, I swept the ground and tidied the floor space, imagining where to put things for the best use of the building.

"I think the roof is actually watertight now, Merrin," Ginny said, coming to stand by my side. I noted the fact she'd not called me Merbin. It was a definite improvement. "I don't mind staying longer and helping get the rest of it a bit more secure. I can get those fixed." She nodded towards the old cowshed doors that lay on the ground outside covered with clear tarpaulin. "I just need a short break," she explained. "And a feed."

"At least I know I'm safe there," I joked.

"Yeah, that seems so weird to me, that you don't have any blood at all. Hey, I think that's why your smell struck me so much." Her eyes went wide. "It's because with other people their blood sings to my nose, whereas with you, it doesn't. It's not that you stink. It's that you actually don't smell... of blood."

"Thanks. I think," I replied.

"I brought my own dinner," she said, before moving to pick up the bag she'd brought with her and rummaging inside until she brought out a small bottle filled with bright red contents. I didn't want to invite her into my home, where people usually had dinner, because that hadn't been tidied up yet, but the studio was excused of being messy by explanation of 'work in progress', so I went with that option. "There are chairs in the studio if you want to drink in there?"

"Okay." She followed me towards the art studio.

I stopped just before the door and turned to her. "Before we go inside. I'm very sensitive about my artistic work, so please don't insult it."

"Don't worry, I'd rather insult you than inanimate objects." Ginny smirked and I rolled my eyes at her.

Approaching the door, I got the key from my pocket and unlocked it. Then I beckoned for Ginny to step inside. "I allow you into my building. Go straight ahead. At the other side of the studio, there's a kitchen with a small table and chairs."

"Thank you for your permission," Ginny said before setting off as directed as I locked the door behind me. It was habit more than anything. I had wards up that protected my buildings from harm or theft.

I saw Ginny push open the kitchen door and then she let out an almighty piercing scream as she stepped inside. The door closed behind her, and I ran towards it, pushing it open and wondering what the hell was inside.

The scene before me knocked me off-kilter. Ginny was crouched in a corner, staring into space, rocking.

"Ginny, what happened?" I asked her, nervous to get too near to her in case she attacked me. I could see no sign of anything else having been in the room and couldn't understand what was happening.

"No. No. No. No. No. No," she said over and over. I saw then that something had triggered her. She was lost to past memories, and all I could do was keep trying to bring her back to the present moment.

"William, noooooo. I beg you." She wailed again, making a sound that I recognised. One of a broken heart. Wherever Ginny's mind was, it was from a time when she'd loved hard.

CHAPTER

TEN

Ginny

*L*ife was good. I went into central London on a Saturday and lifted a few wallets and purses. Shoppers got distracted: with talking to friends, in love with potential new handbags, on the phone. It made it so easy.

There was food in the house and I was able to study, and also be around for Duncan. Miracles hadn't happened: Mum still spent most of her time drunk, but I hoped that soon I'd get her to see she needed help. Then we could be a family again.

Tonight, I had a date. I'd met him in the supermarket when we'd both reached for the last loaf of white bread. He'd told me I could have the loaf, if he could have a date.

Though he must have been twice my age, I said yes. He was so handsome, and charming, and... irresistible. We arranged to meet at The Red Lion, the pub around five minutes away from my house.

Duncan had eaten and gone up to his room and Mum was in hers, so I went and got ready. I'd not had a date in what seemed like forever and I enjoyed putting on make-up and doing my hair. Tonight I could be a carefree eighteen-year-old for the first time in a long, long time.

There were a few familiar faces in the Red Lion and I was greeted with some waves, hellos, and a couple of polite, 'How's your mum?' comments. Lindon insisted on buying the drinks while I found us a table. He took a seat opposite me now, placing down the white wine I'd ordered and his own pint.

Sitting back in his chair, he stretched his long limbs out and sighed. "It feels good to get to sit and relax. I've had a busy day today. How about you? What do you do again, Miss Virginia Bates? Remind me."

I told him about how I hoped to be a vet one day, and how I looked after my mum and brother. Conversation flowed so easily, and I found myself telling him things that were very personal, almost as if I had no control over the words coming out of my mouth.

"I'm so sorry," I said after telling him all about my mother's addictions. "I shouldn't be burdening you with this on a first date. It should be fun and carefree."

Lindon waved away my concerns. "We have a connection. Surely you feel it too? I wasn't sure I believed about love at first sight until I almost got into a fight over a loaf in the Spar, but..." He stared into my eyes and my heart skipped a beat. "I think I believe it now."

I knew what he meant because there was definitely a connection between us both. I felt hypnotised by him, like my world now began and ended with him. Something special had happened and I believed I had now met the love of my life. Even better, it sounded like he had more than enough money to take care of us all. He told me he lived in a large mansion in Chelsea and he worked within the financial services.

By the end of the evening, I was convinced I'd met my future husband.

"Would you allow me to escort you home?" he said, in that old-fashioned, polite manner he had about him. I liked it. I liked that he was older, and not stupid and immature like the guys my age I'd dated before.

"I'd love that," I said.

"How did you get here?" I asked him as he began accompanying me on my way home.

"I got a taxi, and I'll call one to take me home from yours. I didn't know how much I'd drink and I don't drink and drive."

He placed his hand in mine. It was a little cold, so I wrapped my warm one around his to provide him some comfort.

It was a May day and the weather was calm. It was neither warm nor cold, just a day of averages. Nothing special set it out as a day that would be talked about as we chatted and walked down the streets towards my home. Blossom hung from the trees and gathered around our feet, and I commented that I wished the pretty blossom stayed longer.

"Yes, it is a shame that such beauty doesn't last long, before it becomes dried, dirty, and stepped on. I'm glad you share my view that it would be better if such pretty blossom was able to be kept as it was for an eternity."

There he went again with his strange way of talking. It was charming and I squeezed his hand. We looked at each other and shared a smile.

"This is me," I told him, gesturing towards my front door. I'd planned on a chaste goodnight kiss on the doorstep and arrangements for a further date, but Lindon walked me up to the door, leaned down and said, "Invite me in." And I did.

As he followed me through my front door, I wasn't sure why I had, because I'd not wanted him to potentially see my drunk mother. I just had to hope everyone was in bed.

"Is that you, Ginny?" came from the living room. My mum was up. Shit. I hoped she wasn't drunk.

"Yes, Mum. I'll be through soon," I said, hoping Lindon would understand that I needed to end our date now, and for him to leave.

But as I turned to face him and looked up into his eyes, I let out a silent scream. Silent because Lindon's hand was firmly across my mouth. His eyes burned red as he looked down at me. And then he smiled, revealing fangs.

I tried to shake my head frantically but could hardly move while in his grip. Letting go of me, he strode purposefully towards the living room and towards my mum.

"No. Please... get out... leave."

His amusement shone in his eyes. "Oh, Virginia. It's too late. You already invited me in. You can't take it back now, that would be rude."

I had no alternative but to dash after him.

In the living room, my mum sat on the sofa sewing a pair of Duncan's school trousers. She was sober. Duncan himself was beside her and watching the TV while stuffing crisps in his mouth.

"Good evening. I thought I'd just pop by and introduce myself. I'm William Letwine," Lindon said. William? Who was this man really? No, not a man... vampire. An ice-cold sensation ran through my veins. I needed to get him out. What was it killed vampires? A stake to the heart, right? I began to look around.

"Oh, Ginny," the vampire said. "Do you not know I can read your mind? I thought we had the beginnings of a beautiful love affair, but now you want to kill me." He tutted. "Do you know why I really chose you?" He cast a derisive gaze down me from head to toe. It made my skin feel like a thousand spiders ran underneath the epidermis. "Because you are a very adept pickpocket."

My mum's breath caught. Duncan's eyes shot to mine. I gave him an imperceptible nod, as to not do or say anything.

"Pickpocket? Is that what you've been having to do to pay our bills?" My mum began to cry. "Oh, Ginny. I'm so sorry. I actually went to the doctor today and I'm starting treatment. We're going to have a fresh start."

She looked at William. "Now, would you like a drink?" she said, as if he hadn't just announced to the room that I was thinking of killing him. As if he wasn't standing there with his fangs descended and red eyes. Why weren't either of them seeing this?

But before I could acknowledge to myself that the vampire was hypnotising them in some way, William bellowed with amusement.

"I'd love a drink. Thanks for asking," he said, and he flew at my mother and bit into her jugular.

As I launched myself at him, to try to get him off her, he threw me off with ease and such force that I landed on the smoked glass, hexagonal-shaped dining table at the other end of the room. It smashed into pieces under my body, and I laid on the floor in great pain, feeling blood flow from a cut in my arm and another on my leg. William grinned at me, from a mouth dripping in blood as he threw my mother's lifeless body on the floor and grabbed my screaming younger brother.

I wanted to scream.

I wanted to launch at William.

I wanted to save my brother who shouted, "Ginnnnnnnyyyy."

The brother I had always cared for and protected. Now, I'd been compelled into muteness, unable to *move, as in front of me, the vampire tore into Duncan's neck and his wrists before throwing his dead corpse on top of my mother's.*

William stalked towards me, even though his prey was caught in a vampire's web, invisible strands holding me in place, powerless.

"And now it's your turn, Virginia... Letwine," he said, and while I prayed for death, to join my mother and my brother, William instead turned me into his daughter, to thieve for him, and help make him rich beyond his own capabilities.

And I didn't get free until William's world, and a stake, caught up with him.

"Ginny? Ginny? Virginia?"

In the distance I could hear words. Someone calling? But I was lost. Lost to a room where a smoked glass coffee table had become my prison.

"Uptight, money-grabbing, pompous bitch."

The words became louder in my ear.

"Gold-digging, judgemental, pain in the arse."

My vision began returning to the present. There was someone here with me. I could make out a blurred, indistinct shape. I sniffed the air but could smell no blood.

There was no blood here. I wasn't in my home, in the past, where the blood assaulted my senses once I was turned. Here, no blood, safe.

"Gincompoop, you sanctimonious, high and mighty, coffin-dodger chasing mercenary."

"Coffin-dodger chasing?" I questioned as Merrin came into view and I remembered where I was.

"I was actually running out of insults. Welcome back," Merrin said.

"What's a coffin-dodger?" I asked, grateful of a distraction while I centred myself and became fully present.

"I meant a rich man with one foot in the grave, like old, wrinkly and more-or-less at Death's door, and you go after him because he has money."

I smiled. "I don't need to be that desperate. Not when I can compel human men to do as I wish."

"What happened, Ginny?" Merrin's lips pursed, his voice lower, gentle.

And then I remembered. Remembered the table that sat in the centre of Merrin's kitchen. Hexagonal, smoked glass, circa the 1970's.

"I'm sorry, Merrin," I said, and rising to my feet, I pushed him aside, lifted up the table and ran at speed outside with it. Once out on the land, I picked it up and slammed it into the ground over and over and over. Shards flew everywhere and the metal buckled, until there was no further reminder of my past other than broken fragments that carried hints of a previous existence but were now beyond recognition.

Merrin appeared from behind me. He stood looking desperate to assist me, yet helpless faced with a powerful vampire. I knew that feeling well. I dropped to my knees and began sobbing. Before I knew it, his arms were wrapped around me. "It's okay, Ginny. It's okay. Whatever it is. I can help."

"I'm sorry. I will clean up the mess," I told him.

"You've already cleared up far more mess than you've made. Don't worry about this. I can clear up broken glass."

"Okay. Well, I'm still sorry if you liked that table."

"Nope, had no particular feelings for it. Alistair put it in the kitchen when he started calling in more regularly. Tried to organise me a little. Before there'd been a wine barrel. Preferred that myself." Merrin moved in front of me and lifted up my chin.

"My house is a mess, but I want to invite you inside, until you feel better, okay? You don't have to explain your actions, but I don't want you to go home until I know you're all right. Well, as all right as you get given you're a supercilious bitch."

"I suppose I could hold my nose in order to recover in your home," I snapped back.

"That's better," he said, and then Merrin helped me to my feet, and I allowed him to link his arm through mine and lead me towards his home.

CHAPTER ELEVEN

Merrin

I was glad the electric shock thing hadn't happened again as I'd linked my arm through Ginny's. The strangest of situations was happening though as Ginny—super-vamped-up-everything Ginny—just seemed deflated and vulnerable. Her snark had no real bite about it.

Pushing my front door open, I wished I'd had the foresight to open some windows as the odour of warm, stale air clearly hit Ginny's nostrils and she flinched. She said nothing though. Just stood while I opened the windows and moved some clutter off the sofa so that she could take a seat.

"If you'd rather we went back outside, that's okay," I told her.

Ginny's eyes cast around the space. "No. This is

good. All this crap everywhere is distracting me, and the overwhelming smell of fustiness is bringing me back to recent times, like when I met you at the bookstore."

"I am intending to tidy up."

"Why?"

"Sorry?"

"Why? Why have you had the makeover, why are you tidying up your space? You said it's because you realise you need to live your undead life, but only do it if it makes you happy, Merrin. If you'd rather sit and be stinky with piles of crap around you, go for it. You do you."

"What's going on, Ginny?"

She placed her head in her hands. Then she took a deep breath, and she told me about what happened to her family.

To say I was stunned was an understatement.

Shocked. Speechless. Sorrowful. Devastated. Many emotions crossed my mind during the time she took to tell me her story. But mainly there was bewilderment. Why confess to me of all people?

There was one thing for sure though: I'd got Ginny all wrong. She'd fought for money to keep her family, then been forced to steal for a vampire, and finally, had sought what she thought was the security of it.

"You see if I have enough money, then just maybe I'll feel secure again, and free."

She threw her head back against the sofa's headrest. "I can't believe I've just revealed all this to my frenemy."

"A what now?" I didn't have the foggiest as to what she was talking about.

"A frenemy. A friend who's an enemy. Not that we're friends. We made a truce. A peacekeeping negotiation. I don't know what the term for that is."

"Well, how about we become friends now, huh?" I suggested. "Then it's simple what to call each other. You no longer think I smell, and I'm no longer judging you for being a gold-digger now I understand the basis of it."

I held my hand out for her to shake, but she shook her head.

"No? You don't want to be my friend?"

"I'm not shaking your hand again. I got that weird electric shock last time. I'll just say the words. Friends. Also, if you tell anyone what I've revealed to you this evening, I'll come dig a deep hole and place you at the bottom, then fill it back in. Just thought I'd make that clear before we become best buddies."

As soon as I pictured it, me at the bottom of a giant

grave, I began to shake, and try as I might, I couldn't stop myself.

"Fuck, Merrin, what have I said? I'm so sorry. Oh fuck, what do I do now? Listen, I won't bury you in a deep hole, I'll, I'll- slap you across the face."

But I was still lost, deep inside myself until...

Thwack.

I felt at my cheek. "Y-you hit me?"

"Have you stopped shaking? Yes. So actually, you should thank me."

My cheek was smarting now, so I held it carefully in my palm. "Is this what frenemies do? Do they pretend to be your friend and then smack you one?"

But Ginny was pacing. She seemed to have gone from depressed to manic. Could a vampire be bipolar?

"I can't just sit on your sofa, Merrin. I need to do something. Let me get the drink I didn't manage to have earlier. I brought a spare bottle. Can you remove the one I left in the studio later?" Ginny went into her bag and pulled out another bottle.

"Yes, of course."

"When I've had this let's clean your house, and then after that, I'll tidy a bit more of your yard before I go home."

I watched Ginny consume her drink within seconds. Her cheeks pinked up, as did the end of her nose, making her look pretty damn cute. Until she did a large belch.

"Sorry. I'm not supposed to drink it that fast, but I'm late for my feed because of what happened."

"Don't worry about it. I'm friends with Jason, I've heard and smelled a lot worse," I said, trying to crack a joke to distract her.

But she was still pacing, rolling her shoulders backwards and forwards and then she did a few star jumps. "Merrin, I feel antsy, and... full of frustration, some rage... just, generally unsatisfied. I need to do something to get it out of my system. So... let's go to your bedroom," she said.

My jaw dropped open.

"Hang on, that's not frenemies, that's friends-with-benefits."

She stood still, her eyes on mine, pupils dilated. "Well, I actually meant we could start cleaning there. You should always work from the top down. But, hmm, have you ever had hate sex?" she asked me, her eyes now dancing with unbridled lust.

"Probably not in the way you mean, but I bet a few times they've hated it," I mumbled under my breath.

"Vampire...."

"...hearing," I sighed. "Come on," I held out a hand for her to take.

Ginny licked across her fangs. "Okay, but which are we doing? Cleaning or hate sex?"

"Ginny, I'm getting you a mop and a bucket, and anything else you need to get this... need quenched, because I'm not being used for sex."

The mop and bucket were out of my hand in an instant, and I sat tucked into a corner on a chair as a vampire whizzed around the place in what appeared to be a blur. It was so fast I had to stop trying to look. Within an hour the place was sorted and orderly and Ginny was lying on the sofa, moaning as if she'd had twenty consecutive orgasms.

"God, that felt soooo good," she almost mewled. "Thank you."

"Shouldn't I be thanking you?" I asked.

She moved her hair out of her eyes and looked over at me. "Thank you for letting me clean and for not having taken me up on my other suggestion. I'm afraid I got a blood lust from the delay in feeding and then drinking so fast."

"You're welcome, and I'm very grateful that in order to quench your lust you attacked my home, rather than my body. I'm not sure I'd have survived."

"How do you work that out when you're already dead? It's your brains that have to be destroyed, isn't it? Your body is infallible."

"You'd have fucked my brains out. I'd have been very much dead," I quipped.

There was a stunned silence and then Ginny burst out into noisy laughter. Before long she was holding her stomach, while red tears ran down her cheeks.

When she finally stopped, she sat up and turned to me.

"This has been one strange evening. The evening I made a new friend and found out he's actually pretty damn funny."

"I have my moments." I shrugged nonchalantly.

"Let's go sort out a few more things in the yard and then I'll call it a night," Ginny suggested. "Hey, I might even come along and design a piece myself for my apartment."

"You'll need to tell me because I only have limited places."

"Okay, put me down for a place and my friend, Aria, too. She can make something for the nursery."

I stood and faced her with my hands on my hips.

"What?" she said.

"I told you so. I told you she'd be pregnant, and you'd be working in the shop."

"Oh God, you're so smug." She shook her head. "Bet you didn't see us becoming friends though."

"No one could have predicted that, not Nostradamus himself," I said.

We focused on getting the cowshed as organised as could be for Sunday and had the furniture that was ripe for upcycling spread out against another wall. We'd been thorough going through the pieces I had and there was now a pile outside earmarked for firewood. Ginny, of course, refused to break any wood up in case she staked herself. It was a fair point.

"How is Aria getting along?" I asked Ginny. "It can't be easy, trying to get used to being newly pregnant when it's such a rare thing."

"I saw her briefly last night and it's already taking its toll. The vampires at the mansion flocked to visit, wanting her 'good luck' to rub off on them. It's not going to get any better either. I wish there was something I could do to help her. She needs to rest and to be able to give her baby the best start in life, not be having her belly rubbed by people she's never met before."

"I've heard that happens to human females too," I replied.

"Yes, but that's the occasional few. Aria's going to end up with friction burns."

"I can help," I said.

Her gaze probed mine. "Oh yeah?"

"Follow me," I instructed, and I headed out into the middle of my field. It took me a couple of attempts to find the right piece of tarpaulin but eventually I unearthed a statue of a pregnant woman.

"This was a garden ornament that Mya found up at the mansion covered in vines. She said the only woman allowed to be around Death was her, other than the wayward souls. I reckon with a little bit of work I can have this looking like a replica of your friend. She can put it out in the garden of the Letwine mansion and all who want to can rub its belly. With a protection spell around it so that it can't be damaged or stolen, you'll be sorted."

"Merrin, that's an amazing idea. She'll love it," Ginny said, and she flung her arms around me and kissed my cheek.

I threw her off and she stumbled a little before righting herself.

"Sorry. Wasn't expecting that," I said.

"Me neither. I didn't have my vampy senses on, or you wouldn't have been able to move me. Merrin, I do believe I just had a genuine moment of gratitude."

"Well done," I congratulated her, but I was distracted.

Because the moment her lips had met my cheek that electric shock had happened again. Was it only happening to me though? Ginny hadn't mentioned it that time.

"I'll make a start on this tonight then," I said, pointing to the statue. "Then Aria can pick it up on Sunday when she comes to class."

"You really have come up with a great idea there, Merrin. My friend might actually get to enjoy her pregnancy."

I widened my stance and stood with my arms folded. My expression smug.

"What's with your face?" Ginny asked.

"I'm waiting for a thank you," I said.

"I already thanked you."

I shook my head. "No, you didn't. You said it was a great idea, an amazing idea, but you didn't say thank you."

Her eyes narrowed. "You're really enjoying this, aren't you?"

"Yup. Make sure it's a genuine and clearly spoken thanks. I will after all have done your friend a huge favour."

Oh how the tables had turned this evening, and not just the one Ginny had upended and broken.

"Huh, well, some... no... *most* men would have

taken my kiss as a thank you, but of course, you're a weirdo, so—"

"Think you'd better start again. You can't call me a weirdo in the same sentence as you thank me."

I could tell Ginny wanted to lower her fangs and raise her middle finger, but instead she walked closer to me.

"Merrin, thank you so very much for upcycling this statue for my friend. It will make a genuine difference to her life and for that I am extremely grateful."

"See, didn't kill you, did it?"

"Only because I'm already dead or I'm sure it would have done," she said, and then she was gone.

Leaving me realising I'd enjoyed her company.

CHAPTER
TWELVE

Ginny

As I returned to the Letwine mansion and entered my apartment, I dropped all my belongings to the floor and sat on my sofa. Leaning forward, I pulled my bag towards me, took out my mobile and sent Aria a quick text.

Ginny: How have things been today?

It didn't take long for a reply to come through.

Aria: Visitors all day and Bernard fussing. If I didn't feel so sick and was trying not to move, there would be a lot less Letwine vampires now. How's your day been?

Ginny: Strange. Good day at the café, but then Merrin wanted my help at his

place, moving furniture and so I went there. He has a solution to your visitor's problem.

The phone rang moments after I'd sent my message.

"When you have such exciting gossip, you do not text. My day has been crap. As my best friend, your role is to keep me entertained and this... news you spent time with the zombie you hate, is gossip. Spill. I want all the details. Every single one."

"There's not much to spill. He wanted my help to tidy up as he's going to run some upcycling furniture workshops."

"And he couldn't ask his strapping male friends for assistance?"

"There was a need for speed. I took it as a chance to have a good look at his farmland. There's definitely room for a couple of houses there, if he was willing to sell some land."

"Excellent, and what was this about a solution to getting rid of the lingering Letwines?"

I told her about the statue and how I'd put our name down for the upcycling.

"You are the best friend in the whole damn universe. Not only have you found potential land for a new home, and a solution to getting rid of all the suckers wanting to molest my belly on a daily basis, but we're having a girly day. I can escape Bernard. Thank God."

"I'm right here," I heard him say. "You're just so rude."

"What about your constant nausea?" I asked her.

"We'll just share a piece of furniture and I'll sit still and watch while you upcycle. I'll bring a bucket, just in case."

"Sounds good. I'll let you know the times etc when I have more information. In the meantime, do the vampire equivalent of taking a deep breath with the Letwine clan. Only a few more days and then they can worship the statue instead of you."

"I'd not thought of that. They are, aren't they, worshipping me? Do you think there's any merit in a product line? Lucky charms, t-shirts, that kind of thing?"

"End the call, wife, it's time for you to listen to a romantic fairy tale on audio instead of making one up in your head," Bernard told her.

There was a heavy sigh. "I've got to go."

"Goodnight, bestie, love you," I said.

"P-pardon?"

"I said..." I stopped, stunned.

"Love you?"

"Erm... fuck." This was new.

"Aria, end the call. This is not a 'you hang up, no you hang up' situation."

"Bernard, *shut up*."

"Charming."

"Did you just say the L-word, Ginny?"

"I- I did. Bestie, I love you." As I said it, tears ran down my cheeks. I wiped them with the back of my hand, pink streaks across my skin. "What's happening to me?" I asked Aria.

"You're having a breakthrough, sweetie. I don't know why it's happening now. Did something happen tonight?" Aria asked gently.

"I- I confided in Merrin about my past." Aria knew it, her and Bernard, and other Letwine vampires such as my brother, but I'd never told anyone outside the clan. "I saw a table, like the one we had at home, and I had a complete meltdown. I felt I had to explain myself."

"Virginia Letwine, I love you too, honey. Me and Bernard both, and our little bloodsucker. It sounds like it's been quite an evening. Go rest up, and I look forward to seeing you Sunday. You know where I am in the meantime if you need me."

I ended the call and sat back on my sofa.

I craved quiet. Just an hour of no time to think. So I closed my eyes and let sleep take me for a short while.

"Have you ever had hate sex?"

"No, because I never hated anyone before," Merrin snarled, coming closer to me. There wasn't an inch of space between us now.

"I've hated plenty of people, but I usually just drain them. It sucks that I can't do that to you. I can only destroy your brain, so what was it you said about me fucking your brains out?"

"I can think of worse ways to go," Merrin said, staring down at me.

"At least you don't stink now," I informed him, noting that actually he had really nice eyes and if he stopped narrowing them at me, I could probably sink into their depths.

Merrin began unbuckling his trousers.

"What are you doing?"

"The only thing I can think of right now to stop you from talking."

He freed his cock. It was long like him, but it wasn't thin...

"Get on your knees," he ordered me.

. . .

I woke up with my mouth open wide. It saved me the trouble of opening it in shock. Thank God, I had woken up before I had given Merbin a dream blow job and God knows what else.

Then I faced facts. One, that I could have ended up sleeping with Merrin earlier because I had actually propositioned him, and two, it wouldn't now be the worst thing in the world.

Was I that vacuous? He'd smartened up his appearance and now I found him attractive? Or was it that I'd realised he was a half-decent person? Maybe it was the trauma. Like how a patient fell for their doctor. He'd listened to my admission of my past and so now I was having some kind of transference issue.

"Ginny, you are a complete mess right now," I told myself. And to make matters worse, I picked up a romance novel and refused to acknowledge the times when Merrin's face made an appearance when I read about the main male character.

"Morning, Ginny," Callie said happily in greeting as I walked into Buns and Books.

"What've you heard?" I quickly looked around me, relaxing when I saw we were alone.

My brother came out from the back of the shop.

"She's just happy because she's had orgasms for breakfast, but what do you think we've heard?" Lawrie's face wore the inquisitive, yet cat-catch-a-mouse expression us vamps got when we had a potential new focus.

"Nothing," I said, finding Lawrie suddenly in front of me.

He sniffed me. "You smell of something familiar..."

"Soap? Shampoo? You smell of desperation."

"Merrin. You smell of Merrin. It's on your handbag. You've been to his place."

I dragged my handbag away from Lawrie's nose and chucked it behind my counter. "Lawrie, I'm busy. I helped Merrin move furniture yesterday ready for his upcycling day on Sunday, that's why my bag smells of his fusty home."

Lawrie's nose came a little too close to my body and so I drop kicked him. He landed on his feet back in front of the counter.

"Someone is far too defensive." He smirked.

"Someone got too near to their sister. We're not in *Flowers in the Attic*."

"Ew. Though we aren't actually related. Not really. But still, ew."

I watched as Lawrie looked at Callie. "Sorry, wife, for getting a bit too close to Ginny. I don't like her like that. I do see her as an annoying little sister. I was just trying to see if she'd been dallying with Merrin."

Callie stood there with her hands on her hips. Oops, looked like my brother was in trouble.

"*You've* read Flowers in the Attic?" she asked.

Lawrie shrugged. "I have a lot of spare time while you are asleep. I've read most things in this store."

She turned to me, "And *you've* read it?"

"Saw them talk about it on Facebook."

"Well, I never." She turned back to her husband. "You don't have to explain your weird vampire ways, Lawrie. There will never be anything as weird as the fact I fell in love with you after hating your guts."

And there it was. The answer to finding out how hate could turn to love was right in front of me. Callie and Lawrie. Not that I was considering being in love with Merbin. Just the fact I didn't hate him as much anymore.

Lawrie became distracted by canoodling with his missus, and I went to get my bookstore organised. I decided I'd make a little display on crafts: sewing, painting, etc. I'd put some in the window and reposition Merrin's flyer into the centre of the display. It might get Gnarly's residents in an arty mood and spending in the store.

And it might get my mind off everything that had happened yesterday.

The café got busy and that kept Lawrie out of my hair as he helped his wife serve the customers. Working on my display kept me busy, and in the afternoon I had to replace a few books as customers came and purchased them.

One of them was Charity who'd bought a book on making your own wall art.

"How's the decorating going?" I asked her.

"Not too bad. I'm thinking of finishing touches now. I have a lot of driftwood and many shells and so thought I might decorate a mirror or something."

"Are you going to Merrin's on Sunday?" I asked her, thinking she could upcycle one of his pieces.

"I'm not sure. I want to go, but... well... it's a little awkward..." her voice trailed off.

"Oh?" I leaned in closer, not that I needed to be nearer to hear her lowered voice, but because it was a non-verbal response people found reassuring when confessing things they were questioning whether to confess or not.

"He sort of asked me out."

"He did?!" I'd raised my voice and several café customers looked over.

"Sorry. It's just... Merrin."

"What does that mean?" she asked.

"Erm, well, he's kind of shy," I lied.

"Ah. I guessed as much," Charity said. "Only he asked if I wanted to go for a drink with him, but then he said I could bring my brother, so I wasn't sure if it was just a 'welcome to the neighbourhood' kind of invitation. He seemed a bit unsure and so I gave him my business card and asked him to call me if he wanted to take me out... alone, and well, he's not called. But if he's just shy..."

"I think you should go to the event on Sunday," I said firmly. "Then you can get a feel on whether he is attracted to you or not. Worst case scenario you leave with a nice piece of furniture, best case you leave with a date."

"You're right," Charity said, giving me a wide smile. "Thanks, Ginny. I'll do that. Will you be going?"

"Yes, I'm taking my friend Aria and we're sharing a project."

"I'll see you there then. It'll be nice to have a wing-woman."

"Sure. I'll see you then," I told her, finishing ringing up her purchase and watching as she walked out of the store, giving her a final wave.

So there it was. Merrin liked Charity and had asked her on a date...maybe. I could get over my weird transference issue now and look for a date of my own. As I swiped through Tinder between a lull in customers, I realised that them being rich wasn't a good enough reason to date them anymore. It seemed I was actually thinking of looking for love, now I realised I was capable of feeling it again.

Sure it's not because of Merrin? came to the forefront of my mind.

CHAPTER THIRTEEN

Ginny

I walked out of the shop armed with a book on stencilling. I'd thought that whatever piece of furniture Aria and I worked on, I could make it pretty by drawing bunnies on it or something. Or would that make the baby hungry? I had no knowledge of how to deal with a baby vampire. None of us did. It would definitely be a learning curve.

Mya shot out from around the corner, making me jump, and my book fell on the ground.

"Jesus, Mya," I snapped. "You'd better not have damaged the cover."

"At least I don't want to damage a hairdresser," she snarked.

"What?"

"Me, you, bistro," she said, and once I'd picked up

my purchase off the floor, Mya put her arm through mine and set off at a determined pace.

The doorbell jingled and Chantelle stepped forward. "Table for two?"

"Yes please, Chan, and two glasses of red..." Mya coughed, "...wine."

"Of course. Let's get you seated, and I'll get right on that."

With us now seated and Chantelle off sorting our drinks, I finally got a chance to ask Mya, "What the hell is this all about?"

Mya flicked her dark hair and smiled like a cartoon villain.

"My app. That is my Book of the Dead app, has been pinging today. Three times Charity Feeley came up as going to be drained by Virginia Letwine, and three times it disappeared as fast as it was there."

"I wasn't really going to drain her." I pouted. "It sucks that your app tells you my darkest thoughts. Can't a girl have any secrets? They were only tiny little thoughts of sucking her dry. Then I remembered she's a nice woman and changed my mind."

"Of course you can have secrets. As long as you share them with me. So what's the new girl in town done to offend you?"

"She's not done anything. She's lovely."

Mya mimed biting into a jugular.

I tried distraction. "I was going to ask to see you actually, Mya, so you've saved me the trouble. I'm having a difficult time at the moment processing some thoughts and feelings, and I'd wondered if any of your weird woo woo might be able to help me."

"I can't help you if I don't know what's going on, so can you give me bullet points? I have Death's sexual needs, and wayward souls to take care of. I don't have all day."

She wasn't going to give up, so I gave her the shortened version of recent events.

"Hate Merrin. Don't hate Merrin. Opened up about how my family were gutted by William Letwine to Merrin. Told my bestie, Aria, I loved her. Found out Merrin asked out Charity."

Chantelle arrived at the table with our drinks. "Sorry, did I just hear you say Merrin asked out Charity?"

I put a finger to my lips. "She's not sure whether it was a date or new neighbour thing. Please don't mention it. She's going to see if he seems interested on Sunday at the upcycling event."

"Ooh, I'm going to that. Okay, I won't tell a soul. Do you know, I did a spell on Jason the other night for him to attract his ideal woman and it went awry and might have spread to Merrin. I wonder if Charity is his one? Anyway, enjoy your drinks, and let me know if you need anything else." She walked away as if she hadn't just admitted to a) eavesdropping, and b) casting a spell that had gone wrong and maybe matchmade Merrin and Charity.

"What's this thing on Sunday because everyone seems to be going to it?" Mya's interest was peaked until I told her she'd have to actually do something.

"Oh God no. That sounds dreary as fuck. I might come hang around though, just in case you decide to drain Charity again. Yes, that's a good idea, I shall come keep you company."

That was two people I was now bringing who weren't going to do anything to help. In fact, quite possibly they'd do the exact opposite. Especially since Aria was Death's ex, a fact usually glossed over to keep Mya's temper from boiling over. I thought I'd better tell her.

"I'll be with Aria. I'm designing something for the baby."

"Ah, yes, the rare pregnancy. I'm so very happy for her and Bernard," Mya declared, and I realised she was. I guessed this confirmed Aria was no longer a threat.

"Death has eyes for no one but you," I said.

"All of his body parts are for me," she declared. "All of them."

"That's... great. So, to get back to our earlier conversation, I'm not intending to drain Charity Feeley. If I keep having an untoward thought, just ignore it."

"I think we'd better do some work around your feelings. Have you heard of journaling? I think it could really help you. It's not a diary, but every day, you let your mind flow out across the page and write out all your thoughts and feelings. It helps get out the things you're keeping trapped deep inside you. Frees the blockages. It's like a colonic irrigation really. The shit comes out and its uncomfortable, but then you're clear and feel less compacted."

I could just see Mya as a holistic guru now, with her stadium tour entitled 'Shit for the Soul'.

But I guessed that in some way, she was right. Getting my feelings down on paper might help.

"I'll give it a whirl. What have I got to lose?" I told her. "Thanks, Mya."

She shrugged.

"So, are you happy here in the fell?" I asked her. "If we're sharing secrets."

"Yes, I truly am," she said. "But my vampire death was different to most."

She moved her hand across the table and laid it across mine. "I was happy enough in life, with my job at the bookstore, but I had no family around me, no real friends. I was lonely. Yet, when your brother was going to drain me, I didn't want to die. Because there's always hope. Hope for better days. And of course, there were books. I'd have happily read all day and all night then."

"I'm getting like that now," I admitted, and she smiled.

She moved her hand back to her glass and took a sip. "Then Death appeared and I'm not going to sugar coat the human experience of being faced with Death and the horrendous pain that comes with the change because you already know it. But I was given a choice. I could have had nothingness on your Field of the Drained. Instead, I chose to be queen and live in Gnarly, and as it turned out, here I have a lovely boyfriend, a lovely home, many friends, and turrets full of books. It's not like your turning, Ginny, where you lost people you loved and became the very thing that destroyed your family in the first place."

"Did you look them up on your app?" I asked. "Is that how you know who I lost?"

"No. I'm a vampire touched by Death. You can't block me from your thoughts if I choose to read them.

I've seen it all, Ginny. What you went through was horrendous. There's no wonder you shut down. But admitting you care for your friend. It's the first step on your journey of healing. You can't change the past, but you can enjoy the future, Ginny."

"Mya, thank you. Your words mean a lot."

"It's just a shame you said you loved that woman first. Does everyone love that woman first?" She winked.

I laughed. "Death never loved Aria."

"I know, but my joke wouldn't have worked otherwise, and it brought a smile to your face, didn't it?"

"It did."

"Come on then. Drink up now. Then go home and write out all your feelings. Burn it afterwards if you don't want to leave evidence of it behind. It can be quite cathartic to burn it, especially if you have access to Hell in your basement like I do."

"Your life really changed drastically, didn't it?"

"It did... but then I also started living a dramatic life with a happy ever after, so really, I'm living the dream, just like I used to read about."

Only Mya could be given the job as queen in purgatory, with Heaven in the loft, and Hell in the basement and equate it to a love story.

Her phone beeped.

"Oh, there's a D to sort. Gotta go."

"A D? Oh, you mean a death."

"No, silly. If it was a death I'd say death. I say D because I don't want to say there's a dick to sort at my house out loud."

Heads turned to us.

"See, now everyone knows my business. Oh, by the way. I learned something yesterday. If you pretend to shake a saltshaker on your tongue you can actually taste salt. How weird is that?"

"Really?"

"Yeah, try it. It's amazing."

I pretended that I had a saltshaker in my hand, held it above my tongue and shook it. Nothing happened. No taste of salt. I looked up and Mya wasn't there. but the rest of the bistro patrons were watching me agog and I realised I looked like I was wanking a dick into my mouth.

I'd have killed her if she wasn't already dead.

Back home, I fed, and then sat at my dining table with a pen and a notebook. I tapped the pen against the edge of the table repeatedly.

How to start?

My name is Virginia Bates. I was re-named Virginia Letwine after my murder, but it's not who I am. I am Virginia Bates and I feel responsible for the death of my family.

There, I said it.

My stealing led to William coming into my home and the murder of my mother and brother.

No.

My mum's drinking problem led to my stealing.

No.

I didn't have to steal. That was my choice. The wrong choice. I could have given up my studies. I could have taken an honest paying job.

Yes, I could.

But no, it's NOT my fault.

William Letwine was a cold-blooded killer. He could have threatened my family and I would have done all of his bidding. Instead, he murdered them, for his own entertainment and feeding.

*It was **not** my fault.*

Tears dripped onto the page, spreading to resemble rose petals as I faced the fact that what happened was not my fault. We'd been the victim of an opportunist: a bad man, and an even worse vampire.

I felt lighter somehow, and so I carried on writing.

It is not a bad thing to carry on living (undead). To

want happiness. Whether I am sad or happy does not bring back my family. They are lost, but I can find myself.

What do I want? What do I really want?

I want what Aria has. A happy life but one with sparks flying... passion, that's what I crave. I would like to adopt one day. To take in a boy, not as a replacement of my brother, but in honour of him. Or a girl. Someone who has had a traumatic time and needs my help.

I gasped at what I had put on the page. I wanted to be a mother? Maybe it was my friend becoming pregnant that had started this process, these feelings inside me spilling out. But it seemed it was no longer the security of money I craved, but the security of love and family.

Walking over to my fireplace, I tore the paper into shreds, and I set it alight. It took a few goes for the paper to be turned to ash, and then I realised something.

I'd forgotten the apartment had a smoke alarm and sprinklers. The alarm went off and the sprinklers came on, dampening my skin. But they couldn't dampen my mood.

CHAPTER FOURTEEN

Merrin

With everything already set for Sunday, I decided that I'd work on the statue for Aria. The sooner she had it, the sooner she was free of the other vampires making her life a misery.

I brushed it, before cleaning it with a mild detergent and then rinsing it down. It was a hot sunny day and shouldn't take long to dry, after which time I'd carry it to the studio to finish off the rest of the restoration.

Looking around the place, I smiled as I took in the more orderly organisation of furniture, and the pieces earmarked to be upcycled and to leave after Sunday. If I did this regularly, it would definitely re-educate Gnarly on the ethos of re-using and would get me doing more of what I loved. Making things.

I made myself a coffee in my tidy home. It seemed twice as large now everything was away. Even though I wasn't sure where everything was now, as Ginny had put things where she no doubt kept them in her own place, it wasn't taking me too long to work it out, given my place was only small. Yes, it now felt like the kind of home that I could invite someone to, and no longer feel self-conscious.

It wasn't long before the statue was dried and so I moved it into my main studio and began work. I used epoxy putty to make the statue whole again and to sculpt bits that made it look more like Aria. Next, I filled in any hairline cracks, and then finally, I went over the other bits with a little natural yoghurt which would encourage moss growth once it was in the garden. I'd touch up the new areas when it was dried. By tomorrow it would be ready and so I'd decided I would drop it off at the Letwine mansion. I would call ahead and make sure Aria was in. Maybe I could check in on Ginny while I was there? Make sure she was okay after her admissions of last night.

Or maybe I was doing all this because I wanted to see her again?

Jesus, I was fucked in the head. I decided to go back to my house, get something to eat and check my emails to see if any more workshop places had been applied for.

Sure enough, when I clicked into my mail, I had another couple of applications. Miranda from Pizza the Action had applied for a place, and so had Charity. Every single person who had applied was female. I was glad I'd told Jason he had to be there.

I looked at my list of attendees:

Fen (helping) – didn't count

Jason (forced into attending by me) – total 1

Dela, Callie, and Sheridan – grand total 4

Ginny (with Aria who was spectating) – grand total 5

Chantelle from bistro, Mitzi from Saverstore, Milly and Tilly, and Miranda from pizza place – Grand total 10

Charity – 11.

I had one space free and decided to get another mate on board. I rang Nick.

"Hello? Everything okay, Merrin?"

"Yeah, all good thanks. I just wondered if I could get you along to my event on Sunday as there's a lack of male participants. I only have Jason."

"You need male participants at your workshop

because Jason doesn't count as one?"

"I didn't say—"

"What? I have a huge fucking cock I'll have you know. Apologies actually for the expletive there, Connor, and it's true it's huge but it doesn't actually... you know what. I'll be quiet," I heard Jason mutter in the background, through Nick's laughter.

"Just messing with you, Jase. Merrin's trying to get me to go as well because it's all women. I can't think why..."

"What are you talking about?" I said. I'd only called to try to get him along, not to have some extended confusing conversation.

"Do you think it might be all women because they've noticed that underneath the Neil from the Young Ones look there's actually a hottie?" Nick asked.

"Don't be silly. Most of the people coming are loved up."

"Loved up, not visually challenged. You have my permission to get Dela fired up on Sunday, mate, like you do a ceramic in the kiln. It's all good because it's me she'll come home to for the final touches."

I was beginning to feel more like the usual me: awkward and uncomfortable.

"Leave the poor guy alone," I heard Connor's

voice, who was the head chef at Smokin' Hot. "Just answer his bloody question."

"You'll have to count me out, Merrin. You're a good mate who I'd do almost anything for, but I say almost because you'll be with my girlfriend, her sister, and her mother, and no thank you. They don't come up for air when they're all together, and Sheridan keeps hinting about how Callie is married and she missed that wedding, and how she hopes she won't miss Dela's."

"And you don't want to propose?" I asked.

"Me and Dela already know what's happening in that regard. One day she'll wear my ring, but right now we just officially moved in together. It's only been six months. I'd like to save up so I can give her the wedding of her dreams. While she's out Sunday, I can take on some extra work and put the additional wages away in my savings account."

"Fair enough."

"Tell him I'll come. I'll get my deputy to cover the kitchen for the lunch shift," Connor said. "I'm available for all single women, and what the hell, married ones too if they're willing."

The sound of a phone clattering to the counter almost perforated my eardrum and I heard, "I'm joking, you muppet. You've got to be able to take it not just dish it, you know? I've lost a button on my shirt now."

I heard someone mumbling but couldn't make out their voice.

"Sorry about that," Nick said having picked the phone back up.

"Did you just face off with Connor over his comment? As if Dela would look at him, when she's madly in love with you."

"No, it wasn't me, it was Lawrie. Dumbo, with his large ears heard what Connor had said from outside. Anyway, you've another potential attendee now as he says Callie is not going without him."

"So why is that potential? Isn't that a definite?"

"I think Callie might have something to say about him being all caveman and not trusting her."

This was all starting to hurt my head.

"Tell Connor I'll see him on Sunday, and congrats to you on moving in with Dela, although to be honest you've kind of lived there ever since she moved in."

"Yeah, but it's official now. I'm growing up, which is more than can be said for Jason, who right now is begging Lawrie to take him for a ride around the fell."

I lowered my voice, although why I didn't know given that Jase was no longer near the phone.

"Something that's always puzzled me. I thought

dragons could fly? I've seen him change, but never fly. I just thought of that."

"Dunno. Maybe it's connected to his other performance-related issues?" Nick laughed.

"Okay, with that comment and thought put in my head, I'm going to end the call now," I told him.

We said goodbye and I did just that.

I stretched and smiled. My first workshop was full, and any further applicants would be offered a place on the next.

I made myself another drink, and thought of what they'd said, that some women might be coming just because they now thought I was attractive. Was that why Charity had applied? I'd been shilly-shallying about getting brave enough to ask her out, and then Ginny had sent me into a dither. Now I wasn't sure what I wanted to do. Maybe staying single and growing my hair back long was the way to go? Life seemed a lot less complicated then.

And it was a lot less fun, I thought.

I'd see them both Sunday and I might see Ginny tomorrow. It would give me some time to work out if I *liked* them, liked them, and if I could be bothered with all the baggage that came with dating: getting jealous, and people putting pressure on you to get married or have kids. Jesus, I just wanted some nice conversation over dinner and then maybe a shag to end the evening, or at least a really good kiss goodbye.

My mind felt overloaded with everything and so I went and sat on a hand-made bench that looked out over the field. Slowly sipping my drink, I concentrated on emptying my thoughts, and making space in my brain.

And then it all whooshed in. In my vision I saw a plume of black smoke and heard crying. A voice said, 'We mourn the passing of Josiah'. Another voice said, 'We must find the heir'. I saw more flames but as my own sight returned and the 'knowing' faded away, I was perplexed. Because I had no idea about any of what I'd just seen. Not one clue as to the people involved. All I could do was wait until more was revealed to me. In the meantime, I would feel like I was wearing a layer of invisible dirt, giving me the ick with no one else aware of it.

The following day, I woke early, hit the shower and dressed in a smart red t-shirt, and the pair of jeans I felt showed off my bum best. Not that I was trying to impress anyone. I simply wished to deliver this statue and do a good deed for the day.

I'd called the Letwine mansion and they'd put me through to Aria's suite. She'd been delighted when I'd told her the statue was ready early and I could bring it today. After saying she needed to talk to Edmond and call me back, we eventually arranged that I would bring it at two pm and it would immediately be placed in a corner of the Letwine gardens.

I placed the carefully wrapped statue in the back of the van and set off for Chelsea.

Aria greeted me at the entrance and hopping into the passenger side, directed me to park the car at the furthest edge of the driveway.

"We agreed we would put the statue over there, just outside the rear entrance of the grounds. Then no one will be spoiling our lawns as they trample to molest the fake me." Aria sighed.

"Oh, congratulations," I said, suddenly reminded of what had brought this situation about in the first place. "Maybe you'll actually get to enjoy being pregnant now?"

"I hope so. I know how lucky Bernard and I are to be in this position. But the pregnancy is making me feel ill and worrying that someone might harm our baby in order to try to get pregnant themselves... it's an additional worry." Aria visibly swallowed and then gave me a nervous smile.

I placed my arm on hers and as I did another knowing came over me. Aria, with a babe in her arms, and then I caught sight of Bernard in my vision too.

"Aria, all will be well. More than well. And the babies will both be absolutely fine," I told her.

She stared at me, her eyes wide. "B-babies? Pl-plural?" Her voice trembled and tears came to her eyes. It was a little off-putting that they were crimson, and as she threw her arms around me to hug me, I realised that a red t-shirt had definitely been the right choice.

"Ah, now the reason for her pregnancy is revealed. She has been unfaithful with a zombie," a spite-filled, female voice declared loudly, and Aria stepped back. We found ourselves surrounded by around twenty female vampires.

"I can see why though. He is fine, is he not?" said one of the others. "Maybe this is the way forward for us all? We change to more modern times, like those who use other people's donations in the human world. We could use zombie sperm?"

"I'd like it fresh from the source," said yet another and the vampire women began closing in on me.

It was only slightly less frightening than being trapped underground. I looked helplessly at Aria as the women closed ranks on us.

CHAPTER
FIFTEEN

Ginny

After my sleep, I'd felt much more settled, and almost... excited even. Like I was ready for a fresh chapter in my life. I'd had both good and bad times while at the Letwine Mansion and the thought of being able to have my own place in Gnarly, and to start again, gave me hope. I realised that as a vampire some of the older ones might have had this fresh start over and over with their eternal life. Time was so different when it was of no consequence. Things like humans waiting for a certain amount of time before getting married or putting out meant nothing when a sharp piece of wood could take you out at a moment's notice.

What humans didn't realise was that life carried its own potential sharp pieces of wood and they lived denying this to themselves, not seizing the moments, when they should live every day like their last. I'd sacrificed so much for my mother and brother and although I'd do it all over again, the fact was it hadn't benefited any of us in the end.

But it was coming up on being fifty years since my turning and it was time to make peace with what had happened. I'd put myself through further torture mentally for long enough, and now it was time to try for happiness in my vampire life. Oh, I'd had some good times, mainly because of people like Aria, but I'd never allowed myself to be blissfully happy. Felt that it would be wrong after what had befallen my family.

Later that morning my phone rang. Aria. I immediately panicked.

"Is the baby all right?"

"Everything's fine. I just wanted to let you know that Merrin is calling around today. He finished my statue early and thought I'd benefit from having it here as soon as possible."

"So why are you telling me? What do I care if Merrin is coming? What are you trying to insinuate?" My words rushed out in a major protestation while in my head I was wondering what to wear.

"Calm down. You arranged this, didn't you? So I'm just letting you know that it's coming today. You don't have to see him, though you're seeing him tomorrow anyway, so I don't know what you're being weird about." She paused. "Oh. I do know what you're being weird about. Someone's caught feelings."

"I have not!"

"Such defensiveness. Are you sure you've told me *everything* about when you were at Merrin's?"

"I'm hanging up now."

"He'll be here at two pm, and the unveiling of the statue will be at three pm. What you choose to do with that information is up to you."

"I'll be there for the unveiling because it's you."

She laughed and ended the call.

And damn it, I went to check my hair and get changed, but only because I wanted to support my friend you understand. No other reason. Oh that and this transference thing. Considering my mental issue, I called the resident psychiatrist at the mansion and made an appointment for Monday morning.

"Virginia! How goes it?" boomed Edmond from behind me, making me jump a foot in the air. I spun around.

"I'm okay, thank you," I replied politely, while

being not at all okay because if I had a beating heart it would have been thumping in my chest with nerves. What was happening to me?

"How is the new job going?"

"Really well," I said truthfully, smiling widely as I thought of the bookstore. "I love the place and also I've a new found enjoyment of reading."

"Mya said she'd seen you and spoken with you about journaling. I do find that helpful myself, I have to say."

The thought of the main vampire elder who could be the deadliest vampire known to man journaling, almost had me burst into a fit of giggles, but I didn't allow them outward. Edmond could read my mind anyway if he so wished, but he usually didn't bother. He said after all these years he found most vampire minds dull.

"I did some last night and I do believe it really helped."

"Good, good. I have to say, Ginny, that your disposition seems altogether brighter and you appear more settled than I've seen you in a long time. Keep up the good work."

"Thank you."

"Are you off to meet Aria?"

"Yes, she said the statue is being erected and so I

thought I'd see if she needed any help or advice on positioning."

"That's where I'm headed myself so we can walk there together."

I nodded, but once we were through the entrance of the mansion and we saw the crowd and heard them, we flew with speed down to the ruckus.

As I got there, I realised it wasn't the statue that the vampire women wanted erect and in position. It was Merrin.

"GET AWAY FROM HIM," I yelled like a possessed spirit, my eyes burning like fire, and my fangs descending. I flew into the circle and tossed every single vampire besides Aria out of the way. They landed in a huge pile, but all I did was turn towards them and hiss, before Edmond took over. There was going to be serious ructions from our elder. I dropped to my knees so that I could get myself calmed down.

"Ginny, thank God," Aria said.

I held up a hand. "Gimme a sec?" I asked, and I listened to Edmond whose voice bellowed around the grounds.

"Our distinguished guest brings us a statue that we can worship because of Aria's blessed situation and I find you encircling him like he is bait? You." He pointed to one of them. "Explain yourself."

"It was Kelly's fault. She said Aria was pregnant to the zombie and so then we all wanted him."

I wouldn't want to be Kelly right now, knowing how Edmond's eyes would have fixed on her at that moment.

"Aria is pregnant to her husband, Bernard, and any more such fabrications from yourself will lead to your trial in the vampire court. Do you understand? Such rumours fuel dangerous reactions. What would have happened today had I not arrived with Virginia? Would you have taken this man without his consent? Every one of you shall attend vampire lessons run by the breedents and shall revise the do's and don'ts of our clan. We do not attack generous visitors. Not without my permission in extenuating circumstances anyway. Now scram before I stake every damn one of you."

They flew off at speed, and Edmond came back to us.

"Your protection of the zombie was something to be admired, Virginia."

"I was worried for my friend," I said. My eyes caught Merrin's and I thought I saw his own dull.

Then I caught Aria's and she put a hand on her hip and shook her head from side to side.

Edmond frowned at Merrin in concern. "Are you okay, Merrin? I would understand if you'd like to leave.

Please know that what you have done for us has us in your debt within reason. If at any point you need my help, I will give you my direct number."

"I'm sure that won't be necessary, but thank you," Merrin told him. "It's my absolute pleasure to be able to help Aria have a safe pregnancy, and I *know* she will do now."

My head shot back to Aria, who mouthed, "Later," at me. It seemed Merrin had had one of his weird fortune-telling moments, but if it meant he knew my friend would safely deliver her baby, I was ecstatic.

Edmond helped Merrin to take the statue out of the van and then we watched as he carefully unwrapped it. I'd seen how it had looked before and I gasped when I saw the changes that had made it look like Aria.

"That's perfection," I stated.

"Oh, Merrin, you are beyond talented," Aria said.

Bernard arrived at that point, making a quip about whether he could keep the statue version of his wife as it would be quiet, and put Aria in the garden. Aria filled him in on all the happenings so far and then excused the two of them for a moment, saying she'd be back. Edmond excused himself to go in search of the vampires needed to erect the statue, which left me with Merrin.

And an awkward silence.

"So..." I said.

"So..." he replied.

My phone beeped, interrupting the silence.

I stared at the text in surprise.

Rupert: I wondered if you'd like to have dinner again sometime?

"Is everything okay?" Merrin asked me.

"I'm just a bit bewildered. This guy has asked me if I want to have dinner with him and we had one of the worst dates ever. I don't understand."

"Wh-what was so awful about it?" Merrin enquired.

"Shall we sit?" I gestured to a stone bench.

He nodded and we walked over and dropped down onto it.

"He was an artist, and I'll be honest, I thought he was rich and that's why I'd agreed to date him. I know you understand where all that comes from now, but still, I do feel bad about that. He was really dejected when he realised I wasn't that interested in him as a person."

"So what are you going to do?" Merrin asked me, not maintaining eye contact.

I waited until he did look at me. "What's your

advice? What would you do? I mean I didn't give him a fair chance at a date. Didn't appreciate that a starving artist could be a decent date." Oh my god, I no longer believed I was talking about Rupert. If Merrin liked me, now was the time for him to speak.

"Only you can decide whether or not to date him, Ginny. It's none of my business. Just don't use anyone again, it's not kind."

"Yeah, I know. I heard you asked Charity out?" I blurted.

Merrin cleared his throat. "Oh, er, yeah."

"That's good."

"It is?"

"Yeah, she seems really nice. Although she told me she wasn't sure if you were asking her out on a date, or as a welcome to the fell thing."

"Yeah, I botched it a little. Chickened out. I had meant to ask her on a date."

"So..." I said.

"So..." Merrin replied.

"We both might have dates then?" I finished.

"Yeah, seems so," he replied.

There was another awkward pause and then Aria and Bernard returned beaming.

"I can tell you now," she said coming towards me. "Merrin let me know that we're expecting twins. I've booked to have a scan, but given he knew I'd be pregnant before I did, we believe him."

Thoughts of my awkward conversation with Merrin were forgotten as I hugged my friend and gave my congratulations to her and Bernard once more.

"Merrin, I cannot thank you enough," Bernard said. "Given the news of the multiple pregnancy, this idiocy from the other vampires would have worsened considerably. Now, because of you, they will instead gather around the statue. If you ever wish for me to drain someone, just let me know and I shall be at your service."

I thought I heard a whisper of the word 'Rupert', but as I turned to find Merrin now busy telling the vampire men who'd arrived with Edmond on how to carefully handle the statue, I decided it must have been my imagination.

And wishful thinking, that annoying inner voice added.

CHAPTER SIXTEEN

Merrin

Rupert had asked Ginny out again? After everything he'd said to me about how she'd ruined his life. How dark and dismal all had become. I wanted to call him to ask what the fuck he was playing at, but it wasn't my business who Ginny dated.

No, because I'd already asked out Charity, who was waiting for me to name the date and time. One-night stands had been much easier. Dating fucked up your head before you even went out on the date itself.

After watching the unveiling of the statue, I was pleased to see that they'd had it blessed by one of the ancient vampires, a breedent, and she had declared it only had to be gazed upon for luck. Radaya also reminded everyone that all vampire births were still a rare thing and no amount of 'lucky charms' would make a pregnancy happen. She was very brutal in her delivery of the facts, and I reckoned that after a month, no one would bother with the statue any longer and everything would return to normal. As normal as vampire life was, that is.

"Thanks once again." Edmond shook my hand. "I'll escort you safely out of the premises after what happened earlier."

"Oh, yes, okay." I said goodbye to the others and with one last look at Ginny to whom I said, "See you tomorrow," Edmond escorted me to my van and I was on my way home.

I woke to a beautiful day. Neither too hot nor too cool. Goldilocks would have declared it just right for the workshop. Fenella and Jason arrived and we placed all the refreshments in my kitchen for Fen to bring out during the class. Jason and I moved his choice of furniture, a bedframe, into position on the yard.

"My mum's moving in with Stan now that Nick has officially moved out," Jase explained. I'd really like to be able to find a new place of my own but helping in the laundrette doesn't pay much and so for now, mum's letting me stay in the house. She's giving me a little time to sort myself out. Says it'll be good for me, the independence. So I'm going to redecorate the main room, and do this bedframe up, get a mattress for it and then hopefully I—"

"Can sleep in the most blissful comfort," I said, widening my eyes and trying an imperceptible nod of the head, trying to warn him off finishing his sentence.

"No, I can make a shag pad." Jase looked at me like I was stupid, until the penny dropped.

"My mum's behind me, isn't she?"

"She is," Fenella said, "but you sow as many oats as you need to in order to find the one for you, son. I mean look at me—"

Jason put a hand over his ears, "Lalalalalalala."

Fen rolled her eyes. "I was only going to tell him I'd re-found love at my age, not anything inappropriate," she said to me. "I really shouldn't have spoiled him; he's grown up clueless. I do hope there's someone out there who'll actually put up with him."

She slapped him upside the head.

"Ow, that hurt."

"Stop being such a baby and get helping your friend. The others will be here soon. I'm going to fix myself a drink, you want anything?"

We both said no and Fen headed off back to my house.

"Please tell me you've not designed a bedframe that's red or has handcuffs on it?" I asked my friend.

"Of course not," he said, then he went in his pocket and I heard him scrunch up a piece of paper.

"I don't know much about women myself, Jason, but we shall get you dating and... mating," I said.

"I'm only part-shifter, so I don't know if I will mate for life," he mused. "It's doubtful given I don't fly or even blow out fire. I can change to a dragon, but then I just change back. I'm entirely bloody useless," he said.

I patted him on the back. "I don't have much other than my friends and my art. No significant others. You have your very loving mum. You'll get there and so will I. We have to believe. Look how many of Gnarly are now loved up. Our time will come, okay? Deal?" I held up a hand to high five and Jason met it.

"Deal. So how would you suggest I upcycle my bedframe?" he asked.

All attendees had arrived and chosen a piece of furniture. Jason had been helping me move the pieces until Ginny arrived, at which point she and Mya took over. Mya was an unexpected attendee, who then got cross at Ginny for not telling me she was coming.

"If I do this again let's just say I'm your assistant okay, so that I don't have two hangers on, neither of whom intend to help with the upcycling at all," Ginny said to me as we moved her choice, a blanket box, to her place in the yard. Of course there was no 'we' about it. I was standing back watching while Ginny re-jigged furniture around.

"Fine with me. Why are they here anyway?" I asked.

"They're both nosy and didn't want to miss out. But I'll give it thirty minutes tops before Mya finds an excuse to leave unless something exciting happens. Aria will boss me around, because I'm making this box for the nursery, so she'll stay until the end. Also, she's enjoying a break from Bernard's fussing. She's given him the job of emptying out the guest room in their suite and painting the room cream." She paused. "Do you know what they're having?"

I shook my head. "No. I saw two babies, but both were in cream rompers."

"That's good because she's hoping to keep that a surprise for their births."

Ginny's expression dulled and she looked a little upset. I closed the space between us and placed a hand on her arm. "Are you okay? You seem a little down." I noted there was no frisson between us this time when I touched her.

She shrugged. "It's all the changes, I guess. Aria's not going to want me bothering her when she has two babies to take care of, is she?"

"You don't know that. She might need you more than ever."

"No. She'll need her husband more than ever, and I don't want to get in the way of that. Their little family. Such a precious thing. I'm glad I have the job at the bookstore now because that's become important to me. Is it selfish to hope that she doesn't want to return, so I can stay?"

An image came into my mind, and I moved to lean against the wall.

"Merrin, are you okay?" Ginny's face was close to mine as she peered at me. The tables had quickly turned and now *she* was worrying about *me*.

"Fine, and able to tell you that you will indeed work at the shop for a long time to come."

My head was scrambled and not just from receiving such a vivid image.

"How do you know?" she asked.

"Because I just had a knowing and you were

wearing a wedding ring as you served a customer," I replied.

Ginny froze. "A w-wedding ring? Are you sure?"

"Positive. I saw you hand over a book to Charity, and it was clearly there."

"So, did you see who I was married to?"

"I'm afraid not."

She placed her hands on my arms. "If I touch you, can you try to do your weird mojo. I want to know who the groom is."

I struggled but managed to get her to loosen her grip. "It doesn't work like that. I only get brief glimpses of things. It might be months before I get anything else."

"That is so annoying," she said.

"Hey, you're married. Hopefully happily, *and* you work at the store. Most people would be ecstatic to learn that."

"I'm not most people. Like, I was going to tell this Rupert guy no, but now I feel I have to go on the date because it could be him, right? He could be my future husband." She pulled her phone out of her bag and called him right there and then.

"Rupert? It's Virginia. Hello. Yes, what about tonight? I can meet you at *Fauna* at nine. Okay, bye."

Before my brain had chance to catch up to my

body, I'd grabbed her chin and tilted her face up to mine. Now sparks were back, flying up my spine, and I saw her tremble under my touch. "Ginny, don't rush this. Don't predict your future husband is Rupert. Please go on this date with your eyes wide open because it might *not* be him."

Our gazes held a little too long, and then I went for it. I leaned closer.

"Is there a problem, only we're all waiting to start?" Charity's voice had me dropping my hand.

"It's my fault. I couldn't decide on what piece of furniture I wanted," Ginny said quickly, putting distance between us. "I don't want to get it wrong, but I currently seem to be caught between two different pieces because Merrin's confusing me about which are actually available to consider." As she looked at me, Ginny's hidden message was clear.

"That's because until a moment ago I didn't really know how much I liked one piece of furniture myself. I've also had two pieces to choose from, and don't want to make the wrong choice."

"Merrin, you're trying to get rid of furniture. That's what this whole day is about, so you need to let Ginny decide. Let her try one piece and if she doesn't like it, then let her try the other," Charity advised.

"Sounds like a wise decision," Ginny answered.

"There we go, problem solved," Charity announced. "So come on, because I can't wait to get started on my new wardrobe. Although Jase has been hiding in it and making me jump while we've been waiting. He's such a riot."

"Okay, we're on our way," I told her. When she'd gone, I turned to Ginny.

"There we go then. You go on your date," I said. But I couldn't hide how pissed off I was that she'd arranged a date with Rupert. I stalked off and spent the rest of the session immersed in the reason I'd set the event up in the first place. Helping everyone to upcycle.

The day was a huge success and one thing I'd noticed was that Charity and Jason were getting on like a house on fire. So much so that as I said goodbye to her, she asked me if it was okay if she went on a date with him.

"Yes, that's absolutely fine. I'd only suggested us going out as a 'welcome to the village' kind of thing," I lied.

"I thought so," she said. "Otherwise I figured you'd have called me by now. That's great then. Thanks for today, Merrin. It's been incredible. I've had such a good time doing up the furniture and hanging around with everyone. And I'm leaving with a new wardrobe and a date too. Who'd have thought it?"

We'd decided all the furniture once dry would be sent via the portal in my studio straight to the client's home, so there was no need to arrange vans or delivery. Only the Letwine mansion was without a portal and Ginny was strong enough to be able to whizz back there carrying her piece.

The best news was everyone who'd attended today had signed up to do another project in two weeks' time. I made a mental note to collect extra shiny things for Mitzi to stick on her upcycles.

Fenella and Jason were the last to leave. Jason gave me a high five for a great day and went off to start the car. Fen hung back.

"You're not too disappointed that Jason and Charity seemed to hit it off, are you?" she enquired. He didn't know you'd kind of asked her out."

"I made it clear to Charity that I asked her as a friend," I said.

"I think that was wise, given your heart is clearly with another."

I stilled.

"For two people who hated each other, it sure does

look a lot like love to my eyes. But then again, my eyes are old. Though since Stan came into my life, I feel years younger." She gazed into the distance for a while, before refocusing and looking back at me. "The trouble with Joe turned me off love for a long time. Silly really how much we let the past get in the way of the future."

"Ginny's on a date with another man tonight, so I think the jury's out on her feelings for me," I said in a surly and jealous tone.

"Then you've no one to blame but yourself. Why didn't you tell her to cancel the date and take her out, you dufus?"

I looked at my feet.

"Stan liked me for years. I liked him for years. Wasted time. Don't make the same mistakes we did, Merrin, okay?"

"Come on, Mum," yelled Jason. "I'm going out."

Fenella patted my arm. "I'm always here for you, Merrin. You might think you have no family, but my home is always open to you."

She walked away and as she almost went out of earshot, I shouted, "Fen, thank you."

She turned back, smiled, and made her way over to Jason.

Left alone, I stared out over the now bared piece of land where the workshop had taken place. I'd spent so long on my own and yet today had been so much fun. I could do a lot more if I put my mind to it. Maybe do some jewellery classes using recycled glass etc. I made a note to definitely attend the next council meeting, and have it put on the agenda to make a few changes to the space, and to talk with Milly and Tilly about how we might work together more cohesively.

For a guy who only a week ago went out occasionally with his friends, but largely lived a reclusive existence, I was now enjoying company and there was romantic potential.

If the woman didn't fall in love with another guy tonight that was.

But I wasn't the kind of man who went all Neanderthal and demanded a person was mine.

I was a man who needed to know I was wanted... for me. For my grumpiness, my need to sometimes be alone, my fears about dark spaces.

Tonight, I would sit in my house in the quiet and let my thoughts wander so that I could fully explore how I felt about Virginia Letwine.

And I'd see what tomorrow brought.

CHAPTER

SEVENTEEN

Ginny

"So what did you think about Merrin's land then?" I asked Aria, as we appeared back in the grounds of the mansion having whizzed there, although I now felt incredibly guilty about the fact I'd ever had the idea to move onto his patch. For anyone who really 'saw' Merrin, it was clear that he needed his space, literally and figuratively. And now I'd royally pissed him off, if his ignoring of me for the rest of the workshop was any indication. I'd just watched and listened to his instructions of the techniques he'd used on Fen's bureau and applied them to the blanket box, ending up with a shabby chic effect in cream that Aria said would look perfect in the nursery, although I seriously doubted anything made of wood would make it into the babies' room. I'd refrained from painting bunnies on it and so she could put it anywhere.

"I've decided I actually prefer the mansion," Aria replied. "Now that it appears things are calming down on the fang-girl front." She paused. "That's what I'm calling them because they're fangirls, but they have fangs. It was Mya's idea. Anyway, I wouldn't feel safe out here without Edmond close by. I know you threw them off, but when I saw his command of the fang-girls, it made me remember why Bernard and I lived there in the first place. The security of our leader. Plus, he's told us we can expand into the suite next door, now there are going to be two babies. Dominique and Alfred are moving on and going to Canada apparently. They're bored of Chelsea."

Aria and Mya had spent most of the time during the workshop chatting away like old friends. I wouldn't have believed it, had I not seen it with my own eyes. They had a mutual love of books and Mya was 'so happy' about Aria's pregnancy.

"Are you cross?" she asked me.

"No, I'm really not. I'm going to ask for a place on the waiting list for Gnarly, because I do want to be there. I want to be near Lawrie and Dela and the bookstore."

"Is that all you want to be near?"

"I'm not having this conversation with you. I'm saving it for my psychiatrist tomorrow," I told her.

Aria cackled with laughter.

"You can't help who you fall in love with. I ended up with a fool who believes he's French because he was turned there."

"I'm not in love with Merrin. It's transference."

"It's what?"

"Transference. When he chatted with me after I had my 'episode', well, that's when I started to catch feelings for him. Clearly, it's a therapist/patient type situation. Anyhow, tonight I'm out on a date with a guy called Rupert, who could be my one, because Merrin saw me in one of his knowings and I was wearing a wedding ring."

"Shut the front door! A wedding ring! Rupert? Isn't that the artist who declared you'd ruined his life as you'd ruined his ability to paint anything joyful?"

"Erm... yeah..."

"And you're going on a date with him. Why?"

"In case he's my future husband."

"God, you are stupid. Which do you think is more likely to be your potential future husband? The guy you went on a shit date with and who was rude to you about it, or the guy you admit you might have caught feelings for?"

I let out a long, drawn-out sigh, which was all for dramatic effect since I didn't need to breathe.

I picked up my phone. "Hey, Rupert. I can't make it tonight after all."

"But, but... I need to see you," he protested.

"I'm sorry but I changed my mind. Things didn't work out last time. I don't know what I was thinking saying yes. It would be a mistake. You said yourself that I made you miserable."

"Yes, yes. Exactly. And I created the most desperately black, morose art and it sold for so much money. And then I met someone else, and I was happy, and my art went back to normal. Now the critics are slagging off my work and wondering where my 'edge' went."

I huffed. "So you didn't actually want to date me? You wanted to use me?"

"Yes, like you used me."

I thought about what he was saying. He was right. I couldn't be annoyed with him, because I'd set out to use him. Why shouldn't he use me right back?

"Fair enough. I will come and meet you tonight," I said, as Aria looked at me in horror after hearing all the conversation easily. You couldn't really do privacy with a vamp. "But know I shall take you to the depths of your fears and it's a one-time only deal."

"Okay, fine."

I took his address as there was no need for an actual date now. It wouldn't take me long to use compulsion on him to give him inspiration and then take myself forever from his mind.

"I owed him," I told Aria, at which time we reached the entrance of the mansion and parted company.

The deed was done. I'd made Rupert recall everything that had made him morose the first time around but informed his mind he only felt this way when painting. I didn't want his new girlfriend suddenly dealing with a misery guts. Then I'd taken myself out of his mind, so that he'd never contact me again.

After a night spent pacing the apartment and eventually managing to distract myself with a good book, I arrived at Dr Milton's office at eleven am sharp. I booked in at the reception and then waited until I was buzzed through.

"Good morning, Virginia," Dr Milton said. "I have

to say I was pleasantly surprised when I saw your name. Have you come to address your anger issues?"

"No, I fucking have not, you rude cretin," I snapped.

Dr Milton sighed and took a seat.

I slouched further into my seat. This wasn't a great start. "My apologies for my little outburst. I'm just very delicate about people calling me on my temper when it mostly arises when other people are being stupid."

He raised a brow. "Wow. A sort of apology. That is progress."

"I'd like to apologise again for insinuating you might have been being stupid. I didn't mean you. I meant that I last lost my temper in the bar because Cuthbert approached me and said he'd be my pimp. Yet, *I lost my job*, and my guess is he's still drinking at the bar as if he never did a thing wrong."

"You mean you didn't hear?"

"Hear what?"

"Cuthbert arrived home one evening this week in a state. He'd been drained to the point of weakness and then dropped off at a dominatrix's house who'd been given a large amount of money and told he loved anal play, the bigger the better."

I snorted. "Really?"

"Yes. He's fine now physically, as of course he just

needed a feed, but mentally... I don't think he's going to be offering to pimp for anyone for a long while," Dr Milton said.

"Do we know who did it? I can't be the only woman he was sleazing around on. Only I feel I need to high five them."

"I'm afraid I can't divulge the name of the person due to patient confidentiality, you understand. But, to *think* of *anyone* who would be *capable* of carrying out such a heinous act on a clan *brother*."

I smirked as I decoded his sentence. My brother had got revenge for me, the superstar.

"I appreciate your position in not being able to disclose the information. It's probably against some *law*... right?

"Indeed. I'm glad you understand that it's the *law*," he said.

My brother was my hero.

"So, what is it I can actually do for you then, Virginia, if it's not to deal with your temper? Have a think about booking in for that though."

I glared at him.

"No pressure."

"Dr Milton, please call me Ginny. And basically, I'm having issues of transference. You know where a patient falls for their doctor?"

"Oh, gosh. Well, erm, I-I'm flattered, b-but..."

"Not you, you dipshit."

"Phew," Dr Milton said with relief. "I actually welcomed that insult."

I explained about how I'd hated Merrin. How I'd then ended up going into my background of when I was turned, and how since then I had found myself thinking of Merrin in a romantic way.

"So you see, I clearly have issues," I declared.

Dr Milton clamped his lips together.

"Are you desperately trying not to say something sarcastic?"

"Mmm-hmmm."

I rolled my eyes. "Okay, I may have a little..." I separated two of my fingers by a centimetre's width. "...issue with my temper occasionally, but I must ask you to concentrate on the reason I came to see you today. My transference issue."

"Okay. I'm going to say some things to you, and I want you to come back with a one-word answer for each one. The first thing that comes into your mind. That's how we're going to get to the bottom of this. Don't question why. I just need you to go with the process. Okay?"

"You're the doc."

"Ready?"

"Yup."

"Aria," he said.

"Bestie," I replied.

"Blood."

"Food."

"Books."

"Escapism."

"Very good," he said. "Gnarly?"

"Homely." I placed a hand over my mouth. I really did see it as a place I could settle. I knew what was coming. He was going to say Merrin and I genuinely didn't know what my first thought would be.

"Stop over-thinking this, Ginny."

I dropped my hand back onto my knee. "Okay."

"Cuthbert."

"Arsehole." I sniggered. "I meant in his attitude, but with what I just heard, it's an even better name for him."

Dr Milton smiled.

"Charity."

"Bitch." Again, my hand came to my mouth. "Oh my god. She's not a bitch. She's really nice, but..."

"But...?"

"One word answer?" I queried.

"It's entirely up to you this time."

"Competition," I voiced. "Merrin likes her. He's going to ask her on a date."

"But how does that matter if this is just transference, and you don't really have feelings for him?"

"Err."

"Back to our one-word answers. Fish."

"Chips."

"Ball."

"Chain."

"Black."

"White."

"Merrin."

"Mine." I threw my handbag across the room. "I fucking hate this game. Look what you made me do," I yelled. "You've made me confess that I like Merrin, the bloody zombie I told everyone I hated. You're so bloody... gaaaahhhh."

"Good at my job?" Dr Milton said, following it up with a smirk. He began typing into his computer. "Issue investigated. Patient does not have issues of transference, she just *likes a boy*," he said in a piss-taking voice.

"I'm out of here." I picked up my bag and dashed for the door.

"Oh, Ginny?"

"What? What do you want now? My blood?"

"Your phone fell out. It's still in the corner."

I stomped over to pick it up.

"Do feel free to book in about those anger issues anytime," he added.

I gave him my middle finger as a reply as I exited his office.

CHAPTER EIGHTEEN

Ginny

I remained in a mood while I got ready for work, having arranged to go in after lunch. What a mess. I'd fallen for the person I said I hated, which was going to make me look like an idiot, and my crush not only thought I'd gone out with another man last night, but he was going out with another woman.

At work I said hello as cheerily as I could manage, (ie through gritted teeth) to Callie and Dela and stayed behind my desk, not putting any books out on display as I was scared I might slam them onto the book-shelves, and that just wouldn't do.

"What's going on?" Dela said, having walked over to my side of the shop during a lull.

"Nothing."

"Then why are you scaring the customers away with your face?"

"It would appear I am in love," I announced, to which Dela almost swallowed her own tongue.

"This is what you look like when you're in love? Are you sure there's not something else, like a bee stinging your butthole?"

"This, Dela, is the look you wear when you realise that the person you declared a total loser is the object of your affections," I announced.

Callie walked over.

"I suppose you want to know why I look like this as well?" I sighed. "I'm sorry for the lack of bookstore customers due to my lovesuck expression."

"Don't you mean lovesick?" Dela queried.

"No, I mean love...suck. It sucks. I don't want to like Merrin. I want to go back to when I thought he was an unwashed moron."

"Why?"

"Because it's just so stupid. That's why."

"I'd not come over to ask you," Callie said, "because I've worn that exact look on my own face, remember? I hated Lawrie. Hated him with a passion. Until I realised that he wasn't the person I thought he was, and that's what's happened with you, that's all.

We told you he was a nice guy and now you've found out for yourself."

"But I feel ridiculous after all the fuss I made about him being so horrible."

"Every one of us has felt stupid at some point. I failed to believe Nick was the son of Father Christmas. I thought Santa was Satan," Dela said.

We all laughed.

"So what are you going to do, now you've realised your feelings for him?" Callie asked.

I shrugged. "I don't know yet."

At that point Lawrie appeared and I speeded over to where he was and flung my arms around him.

"Thank you. Thank you. Thank you," I said, snuggling my face into his neck.

"What is happening?" Lawrie said, while standing like a statue. "Callie, please help me. I'm out of my depth here. My sister has thanked me and is snuggling me. Could you get Dr Milton on the phone. Meanwhile no sudden movements."

"Your sister has discovered her feelings, just like you did. She's in love."

Lawrie pushed me out to arm's length.

"With whom?" he asked, his fangs descending.

"Can I just finish my 'thank you', before you get all

brooding big brother on my behalf? I worked out that you saw to Cuthbert and delivered him a fitting punishment. In fact, actually, an extra-large one. I'm extremely grateful." I swallowed. "The thing is, Lawrie, that as you know, I lost my little brother when I was sired and it's affected me, a lot. But we are related by blood in a way too because we were both sired by William and so his blood went into us during our changes. You are my big brother and I love you. I need you to know that. Thank you for looking out for me."

Lawrie smiled, showing his teeth had returned to normal, and he enveloped me in a hug. "You're my very best sister ever, and I love you too, and that's not only because I had no other sisters. Welcome to your new feelings. You can now be less bad tempered too, so it's a win for us all."

The door opened and Charity walked through. I hissed under my breath. Lawrie looked at me, the only one capable of hearing it, and he said, "Interesting. Seems I spoke a little hastily."

"Hi all. Sorry, is the café closed?" Charity said, looking around and seeing there were no customers, which was a rare occurrence.

"No. Just the sign of an extremely hot day. The

ice-cream van in the park will have most of our customers now," Callie explained.

"There's an ice cream van comes to the park? How did I not know this?"

"Didn't Merrin tell you?" I huffed.

She looked at me weirdly.

Callie continued her explanation. "It only appears on hot summer days, and no matter how many times anyone buys an ice cream or ice lolly, none of us can ever remember who served us, or what the van was called. It's just another of Gnarly's strange ways."

"Oh, I might have to check it out when I've been in the bookstore," she said.

"Why not, you check everything else out," I mumbled, getting a dig in the ribs from Lawrie.

Deciding I needed to be civil to Charity as it was my job to do so, I headed back over to the book section.

"Anything in particular you're looking for today?" I asked, noticing how perky she was. Even perkier than usual.

"No decorating type books for me today. I'm in the mood for a feel-good romance read. Only I went on a date last night and it went really well."

My stomach plummeted. I was too late. Charity was Merrin's 'one', and I was going to marry another man.

"Oooh," Dela half-squealed, coming over to my side. "Did I hear you say you had a date?"

"Nosy much?" I barked out. "Leave the woman alone."

"No, it's fine, honestly," Charity said, beaming. "I did. It went really, really well. I was so surprised because it felt like I'd known him forever, right from the start. Don't say anything, but I think this could be the start of something special."

"I just need to borrow my sister for a moment. Dela, can you serve Charity?" Lawrie asked, and the next thing I knew we were in the park in front of the ice cream van.

"What are you doing?" I harrumphed as he asked for two cider lollies.

"Cooling you down. What was going on back there? I could see you digging your nails into your palm."

I looked, but of course if I had done, any cuts would have healed over.

"Charity was going on about her date."

"So. What's that got to do with you?"

"It's Merrin. She's laid claim to Merrin." I huffed. "I thought he was my future husband but he's not. He's her 'one'.

"No, he's not. She went out with Jason last night," Lawrie stated.

"J-Jason?"

"Yes, J-Jason," Lawrie mocked.

"Not Merrin?"

"Why the fuck would I say Jason if I meant Merrin? Callie told me that Charity and Jason completely hit it off at the workshop and then arranged to go out. Did you not notice? You were there and you have *vampire hearing*?"

"No, I was pre-occupied with the fact that Merrin was pissed at me and ignoring me because I was going on a date with Rupert."

"I'm not going to even ask. You hurt my brain. No, I am. Who the fuck is Rupert?"

I told him and with a large sigh, Lawrie sank down onto a bench at the park, tapping the seat next to him until I joined him.

"You need to go to see Merrin and tell him how you feel, Ginny. Stop tormenting yourself and get it done. Otherwise Merrin *will* go ask out someone else. I mean he doesn't know that *you* didn't go on *your* date, does he?"

"No."

"You've started to tell everyone about your newfound feelings, and he's the next on your list. Go get your happy ever after." Leaning over, he kissed the top of my head and then we ate our ice lollies.

"I'm so glad that vampires can go out in the daytime. Can you imagine if the myth was true, and we only came out at night? There'd be no ice creams in the park, no seeing such amazing colours."

"True. And I've seen some pretty damn incredible colours today," Lawrie said.

"Oh yeah? What? Where?" I sat up straight and looked around.

"Your true ones," Lawrie said.

I laughed.

After returning to the café, I realised that I could not for the life of me remember who'd served us an ice-cream or what the van had looked like. How very strange.

I spent the rest of the afternoon in a good, though nervous mood, wondering about how I would broach seeing Merrin.

In the end, I decided I would go to see Aria after work and ask her advice.

Walking around the bookstore, I gathered up three romance books that I held in high regard and on my way home, I called in at *A Cut Above*. Or rather, I stood outside.

"Hey," Charity said, looking at me with a question in her eyes.

"Can you invite me in?"

"Oh gosh, yes. Sure, come in. I'm just cleaning up. I'm afraid I'm closed though."

I held up the three books I'd chosen. "I got you these. Pressie for the fact I was a little off with you earlier. I'm so sorry. I've been going through a few issues."

"Oh wow. You didn't need to do that."

"No, I did. I'm happy you had a good date, Charity. Sorry if I seemed a bit weird."

She snorted. "Oh, Ginny, it's Gnarly. We all *are* weird."

I tilted my head while I thought about what she'd said. "Yeah, I guess we all are." I smiled at her. "Anyway, enjoy your reads. There's a really good one there about a woman who falls in love with a dragon." I winked and tapped on the Katie McAlister book in the pile.

"Oooh, I'm going to get straight on that," she said.

"The book?" I raised a brow.

Then I laughed as Charity blushed.

"Aria, Ginny's here," Bernard yelled from the doorway.

Aria came through. "Why do we sometimes still do human things like yelling, when we can hear?"

"Because we retain some of our humanity, although it lessens over time," Bernard replied. "Then we become more of the vampire, which is why I am now so French, mon amie."

Aria rolled her eyes. "Mon dieu," she replied. "You are full of merde at times, Bernard." She beckoned me into the babies' room. "Look, it's a room for babies," she said excitedly. I gave her a squidge.

"You're having babies, Aria. Two babies. And they will be in those plastic cribs. Oh how cute that they're shaped like coffins."

"I know, right? It's all bespoke. Bernard is in his element. He says I am growing the babies, and he is providing. He's being all manly and protective. If I wasn't already pregnant, I think he'd make me pregnant."

We laughed.

"Anyway, enough about us. Get me up to speed with what Dr Milton said."

"He tricked me into saying I like Merrin."

Her brow creased.

"I don't understand. He tricked you? So, he made you say it, but you aren't?"

I stuck my tongue on the front of my teeth as if trying to block myself from speaking.

"He did this one-word thing and I said Merrin was mine, and then I realised I liked him, maybe even felt love for him. I don't know, it's all so confusing. And then I was bitchy with Charity because I thought she'd gone out with him, and it was Jason, and Lawrie bought me an ice lolly, and I bought Charity some books and here I am."

"Oh, my bestie. Your emotions have you in a complete tangle. So, what's next? How will you tell Merrin?"

"I have no idea. In fact, I can't do it," I declared. "I can't tell him because I'm all in a kerfuffle. I'm going to go to my suite and lie down. I might even book a few months in a coffin to have a brain break and just avoid the whole dilemma. I'll ask to be released just before the babies are due."

"Go to your room and read while I have a think," Aria said. "And do *not* book a space in the Coffin Cave."

I knew I was being avoidant, and I knew that while

I delayed telling Merrin how I felt he could ask someone else out, but as I sat on my sofa in my suite I realised that I was frightened of rejection, because my undead heart had been shattered into a thousand pieces fifty years ago, and I wasn't sure it was sturdy enough to risk using it again.

ᖆ CHAPTER ᖅ
NINETEEN

Merrin

My phone rang. An unknown number. Something within me urged me to answer it anyway.

"Hello?"

"Merrin?"

"Yes, speaking."

"Good, good. It's Edmond Letwine, Merrin. Are you free to talk?"

"Certainly. I'm just home. What can I do for you?" I asked, wondering if someone had damaged the statue already.

"Actually, it's more what I can do for you. Do you remember I said I owed you a debt? Well, I'm here to pay it."

"Oh?" I was intrigued.

"Aria spoke to me a few minutes ago, knowing about the debt, and she asked me to pass on some information to you. When I do so, if satisfactory, you need to say this settles the debt. Okay?"

"Sure."

"Virginia Letwine believes herself to be in love with you."

"What?"

"It's true. She's seen a doctor and that was the conclusion. However, she's now in her room contemplating a trip to the coffins. That's where vampires go when they're tired of life or need a brain break. She's very scared that she might be rejected and so is procrastinating in her suite. Oh, I almost forgot. She didn't go out with that artist man. He was just using her because he wanted to paint drab art and make more money."

I paused to take this all in.

Ginny hadn't gone on a date with Rupert.

Ginny thought she might be in love with me?

"The debt is settled," I declared. "Now I just need to come over to the mansion. Are you able to offer me some protection from the rest of the clan?"

"Aria herself will be with you..."

"Right now," she said through my open window. "Come on, loverboy, let's go get your woman."

I wobbled on my feet outside of what I presumed was Ginny's front door.

"You okay?" Aria asked, looking concerned.

"Yeah, my first whizz. Just need a sec," I said. "Erm, will Ginny be able to hear us out here?"

"No, you'll be pleased to hear that all suites are soundproofed, otherwise we'd never get a minute's peace." She smirked. "Also, it means that whatever happens in Ginny's suite, stays in Ginny's suite, so feel free to bare anything you like: maybe your soul for instance?" Another smirk. "Right, I'm off. Good luck," she said and off she whizzed.

I rang the bell.

And waited.

Then I rang it again.

And waited some more.

So then I held my finger on it.

The door flew open. "For fuck's sake, can I not... Merrin?"

"Surprise," I said. "Erm, can I come in?"

She smiled. "How very strange. It's normally me asking that question. Yes, of course, come through."

I stepped inside and I looked around Ginny's suite. It was all very elegant.

"Don't compare it to your place. This is just superficial. I know now that it's feeling at home that counts mainly, though I'd never want to give up thick pile carpets, Egyptian cotton sheets, and cashmere bed socks. Come through to the living room?"

I nodded and walked through.

Now I was here I didn't know what to do. I couldn't just blurt out, 'Oh by the way, Edmond told me you might be falling in love with me', could I?

"Edmond said you might be falling in love with me," I blurted out. Oh, it seemed that was the way my brain and mouth had decided to go. FML.

"What?"

"Err..."

"Oh my god. Edmond actually told you that? I'm so embarrassed," Ginny declared, her face even paler than normal.

"Is it true?" I asked.

"Yes," she said.

"Oh," I replied.

"It's okay if you don't feel the same way. I know a good vacation place where I can go, for you know, a few centuries until my embarrassment dies down. Oh actually, you're also immortal, that's a bugger."

"I do feel the same way," I interrupted her rambling.

"Oh," she said.

We both just sat there. Then Ginny put her hand on mine. Cool to the touch it might have been, but I felt other places in me warm up as the familiar sparks flew. Her gaze met mine.

"I want to be entirely honest, Merrin. When I first came to see you, to help at your place... I was checking your land out, and I was going to see if you'd let Aria and I build houses there. I saw it as a potential way to get into Gnarly."

"What?" I said, moving away from her hand while I thought back to the night where I'd believed everything had changed. "So all the time I was being sympathetic after you went catatonic, were you being genuine, or were you just spinning me a line to try to... Oh God, I'm just another victim, aren't I? You were using me like you used all the others."

"No, I fucking was not," she spat out. "Well, I was, but then I wasn't. Did you just hear what I said? I don't care about you being poor. I think I love you. Get it in your thick skull, you dumbarse."

"Well, if that isn't the most romantic declaration ever. But what did I expect from Virginia Letwine, the tantrum queen."

"I do not tantrum," Ginny said, stamping her feet.

"That's quite enough," Aria said, coming into the room from the hallway.

"Where did you come from?" Ginny asked.

"The guest room. I figured I'd make sure all was going well and then I'd leave you to it, but my hunch to hang around was correct, because the pair of you need your heads banging together. So, until you make nice, make up, and make love..." She grabbed Ginny, and Bernard appeared and grabbed me. "You'll stay in here," she said. There was a short whizz, a door opened and then we were thrown into a dark room. A lock clicked.

"Oh fuck. Aria, nooooooooo," Ginny screeched. 'Fuck."

"Wh-where are we?" I asked. "P-please put the light on."

"No. Stay in the dark, Merrin, until I can get us out of here."

"I can't stay in the dark. Are we in a small space? Tell me it's a large space." I could feel the walls closing in and I was losing it. "I beg you. I need the light on."

"Okay, Merrin. Don't freak out, please. I'm here," Ginny said and she flicked a switch, bringing me face to face with a small room packed to the hilt with around fifty coffins. Some closed, some open.

I freaked out.

"Merrin, there's talk of the wild being around the fields," my mother said.

I stilled.

"Have the animals been attacked again?"

"Yes. Mrs McGuiness has lost all two hundred sheep. Every one of them left like the soul itself had been lifted from it. Eyes wide but not in a passed on way, she told me, but more in a terrified to death way. So I need you to help keep an eye on the flock. You're eighteen now. A man. So you can take a turn with me and your father. We must protect the animals until the threat has passed."

"Sure, Mum," I said. "I'm an adult now."

I was proud to have been asked. It was time to show my worth as a farmer. I'd take over the land eventually from my parents, so I was ready to step up.

That night I lie in wait in the field, hidden in the grass, both nervous and excited because if I caught the wild animal I'd be a hero to all.

But that wasn't what happened.

Instead, I was caught myself. So busy watching the sheep, I'd not thought to keep an eye on my own surroundings. Plus, the zombie made no sound as she placed the cold hand of death around my neck.

"Son," she said.

"I-I'm not your son," I protested.

"You are now," she declared.

"No," I gritted out. "My mother is called Gracelyn and she is irreplaceable. Whatever you wish to do to me, know you will never be my mother, not even close."

"How much?" she asked.

"I don't understand."

"How much for you to be my son? You said your mother is irreplaceable, but my experience has shown me that when offered a financial compensation high enough, minds change. I mean, if not for yourself, what could your mother do with one hundred thousand pounds?"

"She'd do nothing, because you are wrong. My family is not impressed by wealth of a monetary value, only wealth of a family value, of love and contentment."

"Then your punishment shall be that they will no longer be family or contented," she snarled, and she stuck her hand straight through my chest, clutching it around my heart.

I didn't understand because there wasn't blood. She hadn't physically ripped into my chest but had used energy of some kind to force her spirit within me and drain mine out.

I watched as my skin greyed out, and I felt the life drifting out from my body, and then I saw him. A man in a dark cloak standing nearby. Death. Mentally, I tried to thrash and protest against what was happening, but my body had no strength to do so.

The last thing I remembered was that a shot rang out. The zombie woman's brains splattered across me. I heard my dad's voice, "Merrin, hold on."

Death kneeled beside me, while my parents held my body in their arms and prayed. "Are you taking me?" I thought, unable to speak.

"I'm so sorry, Merrin." I heard him say in my mind. "I will be back for you. But I can't help you yet. It's beyond my control."

"Why? You're Death. Don't you take me?" I asked again through our mind connection.

"Yes, but you aren't dead yet. You're in the between. The woman who attacked you was a zombie. Stay strong," he said and then he was gone.

My parents mourned me and buried me, but I was in a deep paralysis, not dead. The doctor didn't know about zombies, none of us did, so he'd detected no breath or heartbeat and called time of death. They spoke of the woman as a madwoman, escaped from a secure *unit, and me as the unlucky victim. I heard everything, but couldn't speak, or move.*

I was in the ground for years. Just me and mental torture.

Until one day, my eyes opened, and my body moved, and I went frantic as I scratched at everything around me until I got out of that earth. When I burst through, Death was waiting.

"It's time," he said. "I have a house sorted for you. It's in a place called Gnarly Fell."

It would turn out that he lived nearby. Death taught me to live a new existence. I kept to myself for a long time, until gradually I began to get to know the others in the village. They didn't mind if I kept to myself for a long period. They understood. Most had their own traumas and stories to tell. I began sculpting and dabbling with art. It let me release some of my inner torment. I liked to create beautiful things. Because I wasn't one. My limbs were now long and gangly, my face thin, my hair long and straggly, my cheeks hollow. I did not look like the eighteen-year-old that was buried alive. Years had passed it seemed. Death had told me I was twenty-three back then. It was seven years ago, but it felt like yesterday still at times. Five years underground and months to push my way out. A living nightmare.

And I was back here now. I could feel it. Somehow, I'd been placed back in the coffin, needed to find my way back to the surface. I begged and pleaded, and then something strange happened.

Cold lips on my own and the words, "I love you, Merrin. Please come back."

CHAPTER TWENTY

Ginny

*A*ria had been so determined for us to sort out our differences, she'd completely forgotten about Merrin's fears.

As he laid down on his back whimpering as if he was once again trapped in a small box, his thoughts were so loud, that enchanted or not, I could hear them clearly. As Merrin's history played out, tears poured down my cheeks. Tears for his past, tears for his fears, tears for my treatment of him. I now understood only too well, why, when he learned of my reputation for seeking a rich man, he had despised me.

We'd been so wrong about each other and now as I looked at him, I wondered if he was mentally lost. If I'd ever be able to get him back.

And that was when I decided. Whether they

managed to break through, or he never knew of my words, it was time for me to be honest.

I leaned over and put my mouth to his in a soft kiss. "*I love you, Merrin. Please come back.*"

It took a minute. A minute that seemed like the longest in existence. Then he opened his eyes.

Lifting my head up, I said. "Merrin, are you back? Are you okay?"

He answered me by pulling my head back down and kissing me like I was his last chance of survival.

I might have had vampire strength, but a horny Merrin managed to hold his own. We kissed, long and hard, and then, when I realised he was keeping his eyes tightly shut, I pulled back.

"Merrin?"

"Uh-huh?" he said, his eyes still not open. "Please tell me you've not changed your mind."

"Do we need to take this back to my room? Only I can see from the fact your eyelids look glued that part of your mind is on the room and not me."

"Only a teeny bit."

"Oh, Merrin. Do you not know me at all? I'm greedy, remember? I want it all." I stroked his cock through his trousers, and he groaned. "Have you heard of exposure therapy?"

"Is that a polite term for flashing?"

"No." I laughed. "It's when you confront the thing that scares you."

"How do you know this?" he asked.

"I got interested in psychology once William was dusted. Wanted to attempt to understand my feelings a little. Not that it did anything much other give me the excuse that my anger issues were justified."

"So how do we do this exposure thing? It's worth a try, right?"

"I think so. Now in therapy it's done slowly, but I reckon I could give you a non-psychologically trained, completely unprofessional lesson."

"Oh yeah? How?"

"Trust me," I told him. "Open your eyes."

He looked around and I held onto his hand as he gazed at all the coffins. "Are there people in the ones with lids?" he asked.

"Yes, Letwine vampires who want a break, a rest. This is where they lie."

"Can they hear us?"

"No. Not unless they are close to their re-awakening, and none are at present."

"So if I really wanted to test out that exposure therapy, none would know what we were doing?" he said.

"Merrin Bruckman, what exactly do you have in mind?" I asked him.

And that was how we ended up putting a lid on an empty coffin, and my lying upon it while Merrin pushed inside me; completely immersed in me and not the box underneath. And even when I went on top and we broke the coffin lid and fell in, Merrin managed to hold it together, while we moved onto the floor and chased our orgasms. Finally, laid in each other's arms, he said, "That was amazing, but I'll always be afraid of coffins."

I reached over and kissed him. "And I'll always be afraid of hexagonal, smoked glass coffee tables. But the difference this time, Merrin, is we'll have each other. Which reminds me." I looked at him smugly. "I rescued you from 'hungry for your body' vampire women. I think I need to hear you say thank you."

"Get us out of this room and I'll get on my knees in gratitude," he said.

I broke the door off the room.

EPILOGUE

Merrin

The next upcycling workshop was in session. Since the last I'd been in contact with Gnarly's planning committee and it was agreed that I could renovate the cowshed to make a storage area and extend the studio so that I could hold workshops even in the winter months. I'd also provisionally got permission to extend my cottage if I felt I wanted to in the future.

Ginny and I were head over heels in love and lust and she spent increasing time over at my cottage, saying she preferred me and Gnarly to her suite at the mansion. However, the pile of books she seemed to be amassing was growing and if things worked out, I'd like to make her a library room.

I'd also had one of my visions where I'd seen a

scared little boy of around eight hold Ginny's hand and got the feeling that he was important. Ginny had told me of her wish to one day foster or adopt and it looked like it would be the case. But I wouldn't tell her. Some things I needed to keep to myself, because I always wondered if one day, I might get a vision wrong. I mean the weird one I'd had about the black smoke and the heir had never been explained.

"Merrin, you've zoned out again. You were showing us your splattering technique," said Charity.

"I think that's why he's zoning out, hey, Ginny? You've had him showing you his splattering technique all night," Jase joked, earning himself a "Jason," from both Fenella *and* Charity.

Fen and Charity looked at each other and laughed.

"I've bloody two of em at it now," Jason said, grinning.

A vision slammed into me painfully. I gripped my head.

Played out like a short movie, I watched as the edge of my field came into vision. The land below—the shifter land—had woodland and also a series of boulders set in a circle, and I watched as one moved, revealing a dark entrance. My sight travelled down underneath, to where a secret cave revealed itself. There was a meeting. Twelve men sat around a table.

"He is not trained as a dragon. This is ridiculous," one man said, slamming his hand down against the table top. "We should let Griffin succeed. He's spent years as deputy."

"It is not the way. Not if there's family and you know it."

"He's a half-breed."

"He shall be given a trial. If he fails, then the council will reform and rediscuss. This is my final say on the matter. *Understood?*" bellowed a brute of a man who was sitting in the largest chair, but I didn't think it was because of his size, but because of his importance.

"Very well," said yet another. "Josiah's heir shall be awarded the trial. Everyone say aye." All did, even the one who'd protested.

"So now we just need to inform him. Get me the address of Jason Gradon," the larger man demanded of another.

I snapped out of the vision. Finding Ginny and Fenella right at my side. "Merrin, Merrin, are you okay?"

"Fenella," I said. "Who is Josiah?"

Fenella closed her eyes for a moment and then with a steely look she said, "Jason's uncle. His father's brother."

"He's dead and they're coming," I warned her.

THE END

If you enjoyed this story, please consider leaving a review.

Jason and Charity's story will be told in HOT AS SUCK, out September 5th, 2022

Pre-order now: https://geni.us/hotsuck

In the meantime, have you read THE PARANORMALS? Book One, Hex Factor, features Mya and Death.

https://geni.us/HexFactor

Keep up to date with all my paranormal romance releases. Get a free ebook of DATING SUCKS, a Supernatural Dating Agency prequel on sign-up

https://geni.us/andiemlongparanormal

ABOUT ANDIE

Andie M. Long lives in Sheffield with her son and long-suffering partner.

When not being partner, mother, or writer, she can usually be found on TikTok or walking her whippet, Bella.

She's written many books across different genres and also writes as Andrea M. Long (suspense) and Angel Devlin (contemporary romance).

SOCIAL MEDIA LINKS

Andie's Reader Hangout on Facebook
www.facebook.com/groups/1462270007406687

TIKTOK:

@andieandangelbooks

INSTAGRAM:

@andieandangelbooks

ANDIE'S OTHER BOOKS

Paranormal Comedy By Andie M. Long

*Books with a * have an audio edition*

<u>Sucking Dead Series</u>

Suck My Life*

My Vampire Boyfriend Sucks

Sucking Hell

Suck it Up

Hot as Suck

<u>The Paranormals</u>

Hex Factor

Heavy Souls

We Wolf Rock You

Satyrday Night Fever

<u>Supernatural Dating Agency</u>

The Vampire Wants a Wife*

A Devil of a Date*

Hate, Date, or Mate?*

Here for the Seer*

Didn't Sea it Coming*

Phwoar and Peace*